Earth Bound

Earth Bound

Avril Sabine

Cracked Acorn Productions
Australia

Earth Bound

Published by

Cracked Acorn Productions

PO Box 1365

Gympie, Queensland 4570

Australia

978-1-925131-10-9 (Kindle)

978-1-925617-35-1 (EPUB)

978-1-925131-23-9 (Print)

978-1-925131-25-3 (Printed in Australia)

Genre: Young Adult Fantasy

Cover design by Caitlyn Petersen

For Rhys, who once thought he could fly.

Nineteen-year-old Brianne has always dreamed of leading a squad. The one thing she has no control over is holding her back. Like the Caelians' mortal enemies, the Terstens, she's earth bound. Sacred Law demands her death by her twentieth birthday.

Twenty-one year old Talon is the son of the Terstens' General. Three years ago he quit the army. He can't tell anyone why he abandoned his life long dream. His secret could end the lives of him and his family.

Both societies revolve around their armies, believing the other race caused the centuries long war. When circumstances bring Brianne and Talon together, they start to learn the real truth may lie beyond the Feronian Mountains, which haven't been crossed in centuries.

*

This story was written by an Australian author
using Australian spelling.

Name and Place Pronunciation

Pronunciation for some of the more unusual names in Earth Bound.

Ailis (ay-lis)

Brianne (bry-anne)

Briant (bry-ant)

Caelis (kay-lis)

Caelians (kay-lee-ens)

Eriens (air-ee-ens)

Ewyn (you-in)

Feronian Mountains (fur-row-knee-en)

Iralen (ear-rah-len)

Prilonia (pril-own-ee-ah)

Prilonians (pril-own-ee-ens)

Taeranelle (tay-rah-nell)

Terst (tur-st)

Terstens (tur-stens)

Zinervie (zin-ur-vee)

Chapter One

Brianne

Brianne Devin reached for the next handhold, her fingers gripping the piece of red rock that jutted out above her. Dust clung to her pale fingers as she pulled herself upwards, her feet seeking higher footholds. She reached out and grasped the top, pulling herself over the edge, her torso against the dirt on top of the natural rock pillar. Her legs dangled over the edge as she paused to draw in deep breaths of air. She wriggled forward until she could rise to her feet, resting her hands on her hips. A stab of grim satisfaction filled her as she looked out over the rocky countryside, her back to the castle and fortified city. A warm wind swirled around her, tugging strands of blond hair from the long plait that hung down her back. She rubbed her left shoulder blade. It felt the same as always. A little angular. No ridge rose slightly above the contours of her shoulder blade. Satisfaction faded to be filled with an ache. It wasn't fair. Before she had a chance to mentally list how unfair, the sound of beating wings had her turning in that direction.

Her mother, Ailis, flew towards her. White, outstretched wings closed as she landed on the narrow pillar. Like Brianne, she had the typical pale skin, blond hair and blue eyes of their people. "I've been looking for you for nearly an hour."

Brianne's hand dropped to her side as her shoulders shrugged, ignoring the worry in her mother's eyes.

"Why do you keep dragging yourself up here? It isn't safe."

She ignored the question. "What did they say?" She held her breath.

"Let me take you to the ground."

Her stomach lurched. "What did they say?"

"Now don't dismiss this until you think it over. Your grandfather had to make a lot of concessions before the assembly agreed to break with tradition. We're running out of time. With less than a year until you're twenty we don't have much choice."

"What did they say?" She pronounced each word individually, teeth gritted.

"The Supreme One said Sacred Law is as important as common law. He demanded the death sentence. He said letting a… ahh… children like you-"

"Abominations."

"You're not an abomination." Ailis reached out towards her.

Brianne brushed the hand away. "It's what he called me, isn't it? Without wings that's all anyone sees me as."

Ailis looked away. "You're forbidden to ever have children or take male lovers. If you do, it's an instant death sentence. You have the choice of joining the House of the Lord and Lady of the After World or teaching in the lower level schools."

Brianne stared at her mother for several seconds, barely able to believe the words, before shaking her head. It was as bad as a death sentence. "No."

"Bri-"

"No. It's not acceptable. I've trained my entire life to join a squad. I won't accept anything less. Grandfather knew that."

"Be reasonable."

"I am. I'd be miserable. I'd rather die."

"You don't mean that. I'm sure your father would have wanted better for you than a short life in the army."

"No, he wouldn't. He was always the first one to volunteer for a mission. First to grab his bow and sword. He lived and breathed the army."

"And look where that got him. Not here at your side, not here demanding they recognise you as a citizen of Caelis. Brianne, be sensible."

"I'm sick of being sensible." She turned away, taking the single step to the edge so she could stare down at the ground. It had taken her over an hour to travel that distance. Her mother could do it in less than a minute. A hand absently moved to her left shoulder blade and rubbed the place where a wing should have been. "Joining a squad is all I've ever dreamed of." Even before she'd been old enough to train she'd pestered her grandfather to teach her.

"It's your grandfather's fault for filling your head with all those romantic tales. War isn't romantic. A squad mate dying in your arms isn't romantic. Losing family isn't romantic. This would keep you safe. And on the ground."

Brianne spun to face her mother. She heard pebbles and dirt slide over the edge, skittering across the uneven surface of the side of the pillar. She refused to step forward. "I don't want to be on the ground." She raised a hand and pointed skywards. "That's where I belong. With a bow, a squad at my side, fighting the earth bound. Not being one of them. Do you know what they say? That you must have cheated on your husband with a filthy earth walker. That I have Tersten blood in me."

"Never. And you know that. Who says that? Tell me." Ailis grabbed her by the shoulders, tugging her away from the edge.

"Why? Do you think you can make them stop? You can't. The moment you turn your back they'll start again."

Ailis sighed, letting go of Brianne. "Talk to your grandfather. Hear what he has to say."

"Why? Wasn't stabbing me in the back good enough for him? I thought he was on my side. I thought he'd make them see I can be part of a squad. Somehow."

Silence filled the air. With another sigh, Ailis finally spoke. "Please. Just talk to him. He wouldn't tell me what it was about, but he said he was certain he could help you make the right decision."

Maybe she should see him. Just so she could tell him how she felt about him not standing up for her. "I'll think about it."

"Do you want me to fly you to the ground?"

"No." The sharp word was filled with bitterness.

Ailis opened her mouth to speak, then closed it

again. She stared at Brianne a moment longer before she snapped her wings open and soared into the sky.

Brianne watched her mother fly towards the walled city, envy burning through her. That should be her. She rubbed her right shoulder and swore. Staring at the ground she began to wish she hadn't sent her mother away. Going down was always a lot harder than climbing up.

She was still several feet from the ground when the beating of wings filled the air once again. A glance over her shoulder made her swear. Hurrying to reach the ground didn't help. She barely had time to move before Macklyn was at her shoulder, stirring up red dust from the cliff.

"I hear they're going to do us all a favour and put you out of your misery."

Brianne ignored him, shooting a quick glare at Zinervie instead. So much for always being friends. Zinervie had ditched her the moment Macklyn and his friends had started tormenting her for being friends with a dirt walker.

"They're wasting their time waiting until you're twenty," Macklyn snarled. "Are you listening to me, dirt walker?"

Brianne gritted her teeth and tried to ignore his

words. Anger burned through her as she tried to find the next hole with her foot.

"Don't ignore me." Macklyn pushed against her.

"Macklyn!"

Brianne felt herself fall as Zinervie's word rang out in the air. She rolled as she felt herself hit the ground, coming up on her feet, her fists raised as she spun to face Macklyn. He continued to hover above her. "Come down here and try that." If she'd brought her bow with her he'd have soon lost that smug smile.

"Why don't you come up here?"

Brianne's jaw clenched as she felt the familiar ache. Why him? Why did he deserve wings and she didn't? "Scared? You worried I'll pound you into the dirt that seems to terrify you so much?" She didn't even bother addressing Zinervie, sending her a venom filled glance before she returned her gaze to Macklyn.

"You're the one who should be scared. I hear they use an axe." His hand made a chopping motion at his neck. "Sometimes they don't cut right through on the first attempt. You're left alive and in agony, before the axe descends again."

She could almost feel the bite of the metal across her neck. Forcing herself not to flinch, she continued to meet Macklyn's gaze. "Come down here and tell me that. Or are you staying up there because I've beaten you enough times in class, you know you can't win against me."

"I'm staying up here because I don't want to be contaminated by your filth." He glanced over his shoulder. "Come on, Zinervie." With a last look of disgust and a sneered, "Dirt walker," he flew towards the city.

Zinervie watched Brianne for a moment, a look of pity and fear in her blue eyes, before she flew after Macklyn.

Brianne stared after them, her gaze drawn to the sweep of their white wings as they rose higher, above the walls of the city. She lowered her fists, keeping them clenched. How could her grandfather have failed her? How could he have expected her to be subservient to people like Macklyn? No one would respect her if she gave in and lived in the lower levels of the city with the wingless children. Even the children wouldn't respect her, knowing that one day they'd grow wings and she never would. And joining the House wasn't an option. She wouldn't give up who she was to become a nameless Holy One, denying the existence of her family.

She stared at the city of towers that rose into the sky above thick stone walls. Most of those towers had no ground entrance and could only be entered through an upper entrance by those with wings. Her grandfather lived in one of those towers and he expected her to visit him. Expected her to have someone fly her to him like a child who hadn't yet developed wings. She was no fledgling to be carted around. There was no way she was going to see him.

Chapter Two

Talon

Talon Morin tried to focus on his father's words. It was all he could do to stay seated and keep his expression neutral.

Barrett stopped mid sentence, brown eyes narrowing. "Are you even listening to me?"

Talon nodded, words beyond him at the fresh wave of pain, clenching his hands in his lap. He was grateful the desk was between him and his father.

"Then what did I say?"

Talon stared at Barrett. He had no idea what his father had said for at least the past twenty minutes.

"You're twenty-one. No longer a child. Do you," a finger jabbed momentarily in Talon's direction, a shade darker than his own golden brown skin, "think you can spend the rest of your life dabbling with paint? You have no talent."

"I do," Talon argued even though he knew his father was right. It took all his effort to focus as another wave of pain hit him.

Barrett continued as if Talon hadn't interrupted. "One day you could be a general too. Don't you want to be War Leader of Terst?" He paused a moment as if expecting Talon to answer. "You need to return to classes before you're too old to be accepted back. Being so far ahead of your classmates when you left will at least mean it won't take you long to catch up."

Talon rose slowly to his feet, his hands gripping the edge of the desk. It took him a moment before he could speak. "Without art I have no life." He turned and slowly crossed the room, each step a struggle.

"I'm not finished speaking to you," Barrett roared as Talon opened the door.

Ignoring his father, Talon shut the office door behind him and broke into a run. His boots pounded on the stone floor as he wound his way through the fortress towards his room, several doors away from his family's apartment.

"Talon."

He closed his eyes for a split second, his teeth

clenched tightly as he continued to run. If he stopped, he might not make it to his room in time.

"Hey, Talon!"

Behind him footsteps pounded in time with his own. Talon slowed and came to a stop, leaning against the cold stone wall as sweat trickled down his back and under the bandages wrapped around his chest. "Marshall."

"Didn't you hear me call out to you the first time?" Marshall looked him up and down. "Are you well? Don't tell me you've already heard. I came as soon as I found out."

"Can we talk later?" He wanted to scream. Punch something. Tear away the bandages and get it over with. Maybe death would be the better option.

"Bellamy's been bragging all day that your father talked to him about training under him."

Talon was glad he leaned against the wall. The pain those words caused were as bad as the physical one coursing through him. "I'll talk to you later." He pushed away from the wall. If he didn't get to his room soon it'd be too late.

"But Talon–"

"Not now." The words were sharper than he planned. He tried to hold back the shout that wanted to escape. "Later. Not now." His attempt at softening his tone didn't work. He shook his head and turned away, breaking into a run. His hands tightened into fists as he approached his door. Opening his clenched fist to turn the doorknob was nearly impossible. When he was behind the safety of his door he locked it and tore his shirt from his body. The bandages were next and black wings burst forth from the ridges on his shoulder blades as he dropped to the floor. His hands splayed out on the stone floor, the heat of his palms barely cooled by the contact. He bit back the cry he wanted to utter as he threw his head back, gasping for breath.

That was his place. His father should be training him, not Bellamy. It wasn't fair. He could do a better job. It was in his blood. His family had been high-ranking officers for generations. He dropped his head to the ground, his wings folding in, the pain ebbing. Instead he'd been forced to give it up. Forced by the wings that had developed not long after his eighteenth birthday, causing a death sentence to hang over him.

Bellamy. How could he? His father knew how things were between them. He groaned. Of course he knew. He pushed himself away from the floor. Barrett was a general. It wasn't just his rank. It was who he was. Anger filled the hollow space the pain had left behind. Of course Bellamy was his first choice. His father thought this would drive him to return to the army. But his father didn't know about his wings. If it weren't for his wings he never would have left the army in the first place.

Talon strode across his room and stared at the painting he used as his excuse for quitting. He struck out at it, sweeping it from the easel. His father was right. It was crap. He bit back another yell, wanting to hit something. Anything.

It wasn't fair. There had to be a way to get rid of them. He reached behind him, his hand grasping a handful of feathers. They had to go. Somehow. He held back a scream as he pulled handfuls of black feathers from his wings. He stared at the fistful of feathers. What was he going to do with them? He had to hide them. Destroy them. Something. He couldn't let anyone find them. His gaze darted around his room, finally landing on the fireplace that would remain unlit until winter. What choice did he have?

It took him several minutes to light a fire, using his canvas doused in lamp oil. He threw the feathers into the flames and the room was filled with acrid smoke. Coughing, Talon raced across his room and threw open the window. It wasn't long before someone was pounding on his door.

"Talon? Are you all right? Talon? What's burning?"

He closed his eyes at the sound of Marshall's muffled voice. "Go away."

"Talon." Marshall knocked on the door again. "Let me in. What are you doing? You're not doing anything stupid are you?"

Talon groaned and retracted his wings until they became two bony ridges, barely visible on his back. He pulled on his shirt, leaving it to hang open since the buttons were now scattered across his floor. Kicking the bandages under his bed, he strode to the door and half opened it.

"What's going on?" Marshall tried to peer past Talon.

"I burned my canvas."

"Does that mean you've quit painting?"

Talon's gaze slid to the side of his friend, unable to meet the hopeful look directed at him. "No. It wasn't going right. The next one will be better."

"Talon–"

"Leave me alone. Can't you understand I want to be left alone?" He still couldn't meet the brown eyes of his best friend. Everyone else had given up on him, but no matter how hard he pushed, Marshall refused to desert him.

"Let me in. Maybe I can help you figure out what to paint next."

"I've already figured it out."

"You have?"

Talon nodded. "The Infernal World and the tortured souls of the sinners banished there at death." He couldn't resist a glance at his friend and when he saw the pity in his eyes, wished he hadn't. Stepping back, he closed the door, leaning against it. The Supreme One preached about sinners being banished there, but he felt like he already lived in the Infernal World without having committed any of the sins. His hands curled into fists and his muscles tensed as he fought not to strike out. What else was Bellamy going to steal from him?

Chapter Three

Brianne

Brianne entered the hushed building of The Earthly House of the Lord and Lady, walking across a dark, polished timber floor. The last of the day's light sent long coloured images across her pathway. The stained glass windows depicted robed figures with cupped hands raised in supplication to the Lord and Lady of the After World. She stopped by the first pew, running a hand over the fine grained wood of the carved ends. The honeyed tones took on the colours from the stained glass windows spreading patches of different colours across the carvings of kneeling winged people with heads bowed and cupped hands raised.

She raised cupped hands towards the altar, which was draped in a white silk cloth, bowing her head before she sat in the pew. Staring behind the altar at the carved marble figures of the Lord and Lady of the After World, she waited for her grandfather and fumed. It had taken a day before curiosity had driven her to send him a message to meet her here. The one place the winged were forced to walk. Even the Supreme One, Elders and Penitents walked. And no one ever tormented them over the fact they never used their wings when they answered the call to join the House of the Lord and Lady. But that wasn't enough to make her give up her identity and join them. No. She belonged in a squad.

A noise drew her attention and she turned her head to see Briant, her grandfather, enter the house and wave away his aide who went to stand guard at the entrance. He was no longer First Officer, that was his son's position now, but he was still a high-ranking officer. He strode towards her, his wiry frame straight, his once blond hair now completely white. He raised cupped hands towards the altar and bowed his head before sitting beside her.

She guessed he wasn't happy with her when he didn't greet her with his usual kiss on each cheek. Well she wasn't happy with him either. "You sold me out." She glared at him, starting with the words that had echoed in her head since yesterday.

He stared at her with faded blue eyes and nodded once. "So it would appear."

"How could you?" It was all she could do to remain seated.

"I wanted to meet with you in my home. Why would you choose this place? We aren't alone here." He nodded towards the figure, robed in dark brown, lighting candles on the altar.

Brianne wondered where the penitents in their red-earth toned robes were. Elders usually only lit candles on special occasions. She turned back to her grandfather. "And how was I meant to reach your place?"

"I didn't think you'd let your pride get in the way of common sense. Maybe I should rethink what I have to tell you." Briant rose to his feet.

She tried to hold onto her anger, but curiosity had her rising also. "I'm not joining this place." A gesture towards the altar. "You can't expect me to give up who I am to serve the gods."

Briant nodded sharply. "Do you think I don't know my own flesh and blood? Are you going to stop sulking and come home with me?"

It took a moment before she made the same short, sharp nod Briant had made. "How am I going to get up there?"

A grin appeared momentarily. "I'm not so old I can't carry my own granddaughter."

The last thing she needed was for someone to drop her out of the sky. "I'm not a child anymore."

He stared at her a moment. "Are you sure? You're lucky you didn't sulk any longer or we would have rethought our plans for you."

She was tempted to ask what plans, but he'd already told her, in his own fashion, that he wasn't going to discuss anything until they were in his home. "I wasn't sulking."

A half smile escaped before Briant banished it. "Of course not." He turned and headed for the door where his aide stood, arms crossed, wings at rest.

After a moment's hesitation, Brianne followed her grandfather, her gaze drawn to the ridges visible through his open backed vest. She fought the urge to rub against the places on her shoulder blades that should have looked the same.

They walked silently through empty streets, the aide following behind them as they strode side by side. The true pathways were above the ground, but Brianne didn't allow herself to look upwards. There were enough reminders of what she'd never have without seeking them out.

Briant stopped and turned to face her, making a

twirling motion with his finger. She knew what he wanted, but it took her a minute to turn her back to him. Raising her arms slightly she waited for him to slide his under hers, crossing them over her chest and pressing his hands down on her shoulders. So many times one of her relatives had transported her like this. It was extremely familiar. She closed her eyes as they shot upwards. She used to feel a surge of excitement as she rose into the sky, thinking that one day she'd be able to do this herself. Never again would she think that. There was no hope that she'd ever be anything other than earth bound.

Her feet touched the balcony at Briant's front door and she opened her eyes, stepping away from him as his arms released her. They were alone. The aide had remained behind.

"Grandfather-"

"Inside. No need to stand out here all day. You've already wasted enough of my time." Briant stepped inside, leaving the door open behind him.

With a last glance at the aide still at the foot of the tower, Brianne strode inside, closing the door. She headed for her grandfather's study. About to step into the room, she froze, her gaze drawn to the man seated behind the desk. "Uncle Ewyn?"

He looked up from the dispatches he frowned over.

He had the typical wiry build of their race, dark blond hair, dark blue eyes and a close trimmed beard and moustache. "About time you got here. Do you think we're going to tolerate being made to wait like this?"

Brianne glanced between the two men, confused. "Wait?" What was he talking about?

"You technically have nearly a year before you have to decide which offer you'll accept. You will-"

Brianne interrupted Ewyn. "Neither. I already know."

Briant pointed a finger at her. "Sit down, shut up and listen. And stop jumping to conclusions. This is bigger than you, Sprite."

Brianne sat on the stool. His use of her childhood nickname stopped her from arguing. "I'm listening." She bit back the words, and this had better be good.

Ewyn stared at her a moment before he gave the same sharp, short nod he had picked up from his father. "Every time we send out a squad, the Terstens are waiting for them. Every. Time." The base of his fist hit the desk in time with his last two words. "We always know where they plan to attack. Merchants stumble across information, people are captured, information arrives mysteriously. Every single time we somehow find out when they'll attack and we are there waiting for them."

"It isn't natural," Briant said.

Brianne frowned. "It's good, isn't it? Knowing when they're going to attack." How could they be upset that they always found out in time to stop the Terstens?

"So you'd think." Ewyn slid a piece of paper towards her. "The last battle."

She read the names of the deceased. Nine names. Only one would have survived from that squad. She looked up at her uncle. "I don't understand."

"Seven years ago we changed from five in a squad to ten. So did they." Ewyn pointed to the paper she still held. "These days we're so evenly matched that only one soldier survives each battle. One of ours or one of theirs. Every single time."

"We're trained to fight to the death." Brianne still couldn't figure out what the point was.

"We need an advantage. One no one else knows about," Briant said.

"No one knows-" she broke off mid sentence as it finally dawned on her. "We have a spy passing along information?"

Briant shrugged. "We have a lot of coincidences. We're matching each other battle for battle. No one is advancing. We even sent out a squad under the flag of truce, but they were all slaughtered. We need a spy to infiltrate the enemy and see what they can discover. Someone that only we will know about."

"How can-" again she broke off, her hand going to her shoulder blade. "Oh."

Briant nodded. "Yes. Oh."

Her hand reached up to touch the waves of blond hair that fell halfway down her back. "Impossible. I don't look anything like them. They're all dark haired, dark eyed and dark skinned."

Ewyn placed a leather pouch on the desk between them. "Nothing is impossible." When she didn't take it, he pushed it towards her.

She slowly reached out and undid the drawstring, tipping the dried berries into her hand. She dropped them on the table, bringing her hand to her chest, the other gripping the edge of the desk. "They're poisonous."

"Not really. It takes years of eating them before they kill you. They'll make you infertile if you take them for about a year, but that isn't a problem for you. The Supreme One will have you killed if you even think about breeding." Ewyn gestured towards the berries. "A week of taking those and your skin and eyes will darken and your hair will start to grow out dark."

"You'll have to cut your hair short. All their soldiers have short hair," Briant said.

Her hand reached up to her hair again. "How short?"

Briant leaned towards her, his hands pressed against the desk. "You have three choices. Stop worrying about inconsequential things. Do you want to teach fledglings?"

Brianne met his gaze, rising to her feet. "No. You know I don't."

"We'll tell everyone you've retreated to the coast to think about what you're going to do. We'll stash you by the border and get word to you when an opportunity presents itself." Briant met her stare.

Ewyn scooped up the berries. "You'll start taking these and cut your hair close. We'll give you dye to use. Trim the dyed ends when it starts growing in dark and then you wont have to worry about dye." He held the berries out to her.

Trim the ends when it started growing in? How long did they expect her to spy for them? Fear and excitement rushed through her. She'd trained forever to be in a squad. To take to the air with a bow and fight to protect her country. Fight to take back the land the Terstens had stolen from them. They'd come over the mountains centuries ago and stolen their fertile lands, leaving them a barren country.

She had dreamed of being a soldier, not a spy. Her gaze was drawn to the berries. A spy was a thousand times better than becoming a penitent or teacher. And she'd still be protecting her people, which is what she would have done if she'd become a soldier. Reaching out, she took the berries, meeting Ewyn's gaze as she popped three of them into her mouth. Bitterness made her wince and she took the glass of water her grandfather held out to her.

"We have a lot of preparations to make." Ewyn handed her the leather pouch to put the remaining berries in. "First you need to meet my new aide. I believe you were in class together until he gained his wings." Ewyn opened a second door in the room and gestured someone forward.

Brianne barely kept from gaping when Macklyn stepped into the room with a grin. "He's your aide?" It was an effort to keep her voice neutral.

Ewyn nodded sharply. "Yesterday. He's the best in his class, comes from a well placed family and shows potential."

Brianne's hands curled into fists. Best in his class! Only once he'd left the class they'd both attended. Until then he'd been second best. The bitterness she tasted this time couldn't be washed away with a glass of water. "I thought you didn't want a lot of people knowing about this."

"Only the four of us," Ewyn said.

"I'll be your transport." Macklyn smiled.

She could almost hear the words dirt walker at the end of his comment and wanted to knock the smile off his face. Instead, she dredged up her own insincere smile. "I'm glad they finally found a use for you." Her smile widened as Macklyn's faded.

"I want you both back here tomorrow at the same time, but before then, you need to practice flying together," Ewyn said.

"Unsupervised?" Brianne nearly took a step back at the smile that returned to Macklyn's face.

"We're trying to keep this quiet. Get out in the desert. Alone," Briant said.

Brianne shook her head. "Then people will talk. There's no way they'll think we've suddenly become friends." She itched to slam her fist into his smiling mouth.

"She's right, sir. No one would believe we're friends. When I moved onto the next class without her, she started trying to pick fights with me."

Her hands curled into fists. She'd show him all

about picking fights with someone. It took every bit of willpower not to hit him.

"Then the pair of you had better figure something out. This mission hinges on the two of you spending time together without raising suspicion," Briant ordered.

Brianne opened her mouth to say impossible, but smiled instead. "I can think of one reason people would believe we're spending time together. Only if it was an order."

"Come up with a better idea. There's no reason for us to order that," Ewyn said.

Brianne continued to smile. "You would if you caught us brawling."

Briant chuckled, turning to Ewyn. "See, quick on her feet. She'll manage."

"She better. Ailis will have both our hides if she doesn't come back in one piece and she found out the reason why."

Chapter Four

Talon

Talon stared at the summons in his hand, wanting to tear the paper into pieces. He'd managed to avoid his father for two days, this he couldn't ignore. "Tell him I'll be there soon."

"But-" the boy's words stopped when Talon shut the door in his face.

He ignored the knocking on his door as he locked it and strode to his bed where he dropped the summons. Once his shirt was unbuttoned, it and the bandages joined the paper. After several deep breaths, his wings rose from his back and he winced at the pain as they stretched, his hands curling into fists. There had to be a way to get rid of them. He couldn't keep doing this. Hiding in his room or keeping them bound so they couldn't escape and betray him.

Letting them out, when they were long past cramped and pain arrowed through his body, was becoming more difficult every day. There had to be some way to be rid of them.

It took several minutes of concentration before he finally forced them to retract. He wrapped the bandages around his chest, hiding the bony ridges and preventing his wings from escaping.

As soon as his shirt was buttoned, he strode towards his father's office to find Bellamy waiting in the corridor. With a daggered look at Bellamy, Talon flung open the door and strode inside, slamming the door shut behind him. He stood at the desk, staring at his father's bent head as he scrawled line after line on an open book.

When Talon was about to demand his father's attention, he finally looked up, placing the pen beside the book. "Sit down, Talon." He gestured towards the chair in front of him.

Talon continued to stand. "You wanted to see me?"

"Sit down." This time the words were a command.

Talon ignored them. "Will this take long? I'm in the middle of a painting that's going really well." The disappointed look his father gave him made him want to take the words back, but he couldn't.

Barrett rose to his feet. "It's well past time I choose a replacement for Farren."

Talon nodded slowly. He knew this moment had to come. Farren, his father's cousin, had died in battle several months ago and should have been replaced well before this. "He will be missed."

Barrett slammed his hands against the desk. "I didn't bring you here for platitudes. I want you to captain his unit under my guidance and continue with your training."

"I'm not in the army anymore." Once he would have begged for the chance to be a unit captain.

"Don't give me that rubbish. A two-year-old could paint better than you."

He wanted to argue, but every word was true and he was sick of explaining himself. It was impossible to keep his wings retracted all the time. What other excuse could he use for shutting himself away in his room for hours on end, sometimes days? All he could do was meet his father's glare.

"Well? When are you going to forget this stupidity and return to the army?" Barrett made a jabbing gesture towards the door. "Or do I offer the position to someone else?"

He didn't need to be told who that someone else

was. Hands curled into fists and his jaw tightened as he held back the words he wanted to speak.

"Well?"

Talon's words were soft, the anger barely held at bay. "I can't live without my art."

"Then do it as a hobby." The words were sharp, the stare cutting.

His father wouldn't understand and he couldn't explain. If Barrett knew, he not only risked his livelihood as War Leader of his people, but also his life for letting Talon live. Talon didn't know what his father would do. Save his son or keep his position by accusing him of having wings.

"Are you even paying attention to me?"

"Are you paying attention to me?"

Barrett pointed a finger at his son. "This is your last chance. You walk out that door," his finger aimed at the door, "And you are nothing. Do you understand? Nothing. Your art can't do for you what this position can."

Talon could only nod. More than anything else he wanted to captain his own unit. To be trained by his father, in the hope of becoming the next War Leader of Terst.

"Well?"

"Without my art, I can't live." He turned away, staring at the door several steps away, unable to move.

"Send Bellamy in."

His eyes closed at the pain those words caused. Then he realised it was physical pain. Even after taking the time to stretch his wings, they wanted to break free. He hurried forward, the pain increasing as he flung open the door. Leaving the door open, he strode towards his room, not bothering to pass on the message.

He hadn't needed to. Behind him he heard his father roar Bellamy's name and he broke into a run. That was his place. Bellamy was stealing his position, stealing everything he'd always wanted.

Reaching his room, Talon flung his door open, stepping out of the way as it crashed closed. Locking the door, he tore his shirt from his body, flinging it and the bandages to the ground as he sank to his knees. He fell forward, his hands colliding with the stone floor as black wings rose up around him. A sound drew his head up, his teeth clenched tight as he fought against the pain. His fifteen-year-old sister stood beside the window, mouth open, shock in her brown eyes.

"Talon?" She took a step forward, a hand outstretched.

"Garnet." He struggled to his feet, trying desperately to retract his wings. They wouldn't obey, remaining around him like an unwanted cloak.

She shook her head, straight black hair flying around her face and shoulders. "No. Not you. I can't lose you." She ran towards him and threw her arms around him.

"Garnet-" he broke off the assurances that would have been lies, enfolding her in his arms. "I'm sorry." He felt her tears against his bare chest and his arms tightened. "Shh Garnet. Shh."

"They'll kill you."

"One day. But not until they know."

She tilted her head upwards, tears staining her cheeks, her brown eyes filled with more. "How long?"

"When I was eighteen."

Her mouth opened, closed and opened again. "When you quit the army. Oh Talon." She buried her head against his chest again.

"Shh." Her pain was tearing him apart. If he'd had the strength he would have ended it all before now instead of risking his family being sentenced with him.

Again she looked up at him. "We have to do something. Can't we get rid of them?"

"Do you think I haven't tried?"

"Does our father know?"

"No." The word came out sharper than he planned.

"Anyone?"

"No."

"Why? Why you?"

He had no answer for her. It was a question he'd asked a million times and never once had he received an answer. "When I'm caught, you have to deny you ever knew. They'd kill you too." He wished he could tell her it would be safer for her to turn him in, but he couldn't. He didn't want to die. Facing death in battle was different from being hung like a criminal.

Chapter Five

Brianne

Brianne ran a hand over her head again. The stubble felt strange after having long hair her entire life. A sound had her reaching for the bow, which hung at her back. She grabbed an arrow with her other hand as she spun to see Macklyn flying towards her. Lowering the bow she continued to hold it and the arrow as he flew towards her, a sack in his hands.

She ran her tongue over the almost healed split in her upper lip, smiling slightly at the memory of her fight with Macklyn. A pity they'd dragged them apart so soon, but at least she'd managed to blacken his eye and cause more damage than the single split lip he'd given her.

As Macklyn landed in the gully, she squinted her eyes against the red dust that swirled around them from the dry, cracked earth and the pillars of stone that created the perfect hiding place. Brianne fought the temptation to put the arrow to the string of the bow and draw it back. She hated how she relied on Macklyn to bring her food and keep her informed of what was happening. The past nine days had dragged.

Macklyn dropped the sack at her feet. "You've got ten minutes to eat and get ready. It's time."

"Time?" Her heart raced as she waited for him to clarify his comment.

"We won a battle. First Officer Ewyn is at the scene preparing things now."

As much as she hated to, Brianne knelt at his feet to pick up the sack, quickly rising. She pulled out the flatbread, unwrapped it and took a bite as she checked the other contents. More vieteh berries, blood stained clothes, worn boots and a curved dagger. She looked up at Macklyn with a question in her eyes.

"They were taken from a soldier similar to your size. Hurry up, you don't want to mess this up and have one of their patrols find the battle site before you get there."

With a sharp nod, Brianne ate the last of the flatbread then hurried behind a stone pillar to dress in the unknown soldier's clothes. Some of the blood was still damp and she tried not to think about it as she sat down to pull on the boots. They were only slightly big on her. Once the dagger was tucked inside one boot and the berries in her belt pouch, she returned to Macklyn. "I'm ready."

He nodded to the bundle of clothes and her bow and quiver she also carried. "First Officer Ewyn said you're to take nothing personal. Leave that here and I'll collect them after I drop you off."

Her grip tightened on her bow. She didn't trust him. "Wait here." Striding between the rock pillars, checking over her shoulder that she was hidden from Macklyn's view, she headed for the small cave she'd found in a dead end canyon during her wanderings while she'd waited for orders. She hid her gear amongst some loose rubble and pushed dirt over them. Crawling out of the cave, she dusted off her borrowed clothes before she returned to Macklyn. He was still where she'd left him.

He turned towards her, having kicked dirt over the fire pit to smother the glowing embers. "Can we go now?"

As much as she hated to, Brianne turned her back to him, holding her arms slightly away from her sides. She felt Macklyn come up behind her and had to force herself to remain relaxed. His arms encircled her, crossing over her chest so his hands could grasp her shoulders. He launched into the air and Brianne felt the familiar anger rush through her.

She should be able to do this. It wasn't fair that she was forced to be carted around like a little child, a fledgling yet to grow wings. The air rushed at her, the land flying beneath them until they reached their destination. They descended to the ground, which was littered with bodies, the earth stained by blood darker than the red of the earth.

Ewyn strode to meet them, an unsheathed sword in his hands. "Remember to take the vieteh berries every day. Don't forget even once. If they ask why you take them say you're devoting your life to the army and your country and don't want to have children."

Brianne nodded, trying not to think about the long-term effects. A year and it would be true, she'd never be able to have children. She hoped this mission didn't take that long, but maybe she should keep taking them anyway. Did she really want to bring more abominations into the world?

"I had hoped to have time to go over the plan with you again."

She stood straight. "I remember every bit of it, sir." It was simple enough. Find out where the information was coming from. The rest of the plan was possibilities and suggestions.

Ewyn nodded sharply. "Try and get away by yourself as soon as possible. Macklyn will keep track of your movements and find a way to meet up with you. But don't make them suspicious. We want you to stay there as long as possible."

"Yes, sir."

Ewyn turned to Macklyn. "Make it look believable but don't damage her." He again turned to Brianne and handed her the sword. "This is yours. The soldier also had a crossbow, but it's broken." He momentarily rested a hand on her shoulder before he kissed each of her cheeks. "Good luck." His gaze travelled from one to the other. "I'll scout the area and make sure we're still safe." He launched into the air.

"I'm going to enjoy this."

Brianne started to turn towards Macklyn to ask him what he'd enjoy. She barely caught a glimpse of his grin and a raised sword before her head exploded and the world went black.

Chapter Six

Talon

Talon stared at a curved dagger. His hand tightened on the handle and he took a deep breath before he raised his gaze to the mirror he stood before. Wings rose around him and steeling himself, he reached back with the dagger, aiming for where his flesh became wing.

A pounding on his door froze his hand, the dagger less than an inch from his skin. He forced himself to ignore the pounding and took another deep breath.

"Talon!"

He closed his eyes and lowered the dagger. Marshall never gave up.

"Talon. Let me in."

It took him a few minutes before he could retract his wings, the task not made easier by Marshall calling to him again and knocking on the door a couple of times. Returning his dagger to his boot, Talon scooped up his shirt and kicked the bandages under the bed. He strode to the door, hurriedly buttoning his shirt, as Marshall pounded on the door again.

He flung the door open to find Marshall with fist raised. "What?"

"Let me in."

"What do you want, Marshall?"

Marshall's gaze dropped to the ground and he ran a hand through his hair, the black strands the maximum length of five inches the army allowed. He gestured past Talon. "Look out your window."

Talon started to close the door.

"Oh come on, Talon. What have you got hidden in there?" Marshall reached out a hand to stop the door closing.

Talon glanced past Marshall and saw several people walking down the corridor towards them. He opened the door wider. "Hurry up then." He slammed the door behind Marshall, automatically locking it before he strode to the window.

As his gaze was drawn to the back road, the one the army used to avoid travelling through the city, he felt like someone had punched him in the stomach. Riding beside his father was Bellamy, leather armour, sword at his side, crossbow hooked onto his saddle. Talon's hands tightened on the window ledge, knuckles white. That should have been him.

"Why?"

Still gripping the ledge, Talon looked towards Marshall. If he let go, he didn't know what he'd do.

"Why, Talon? Why quit?" He waved a hand towards the window. "And don't tell me that doesn't bother you. I know you. No matter how much you try and push us all away, I still know you. Why did you quit?"

"Drop it. Just drop it." His words were harsh.

"You're not a painter. You'd never even thought about being a painter until you randomly decided to quit three years ago. Why. Tell me. You know I won't judge you. When have I ever?"

"I can't."

"Can't what? Be in the army? I've tried to understand. Tried to stand up for you, but you won't even tell me. Why?"

Talon shook his head, tempted to spill the secret Garnet now knew. But he couldn't risk his friend's life like that. It was bad enough Garnet knew. "I can't."

"Was it your first battle? I won't think less of you if that was it."

Talon shook his head again. This time he couldn't speak. It hadn't been battle fear, it had been fear that if he'd been injured someone would have discovered his secret. He'd thought he could continue to hide what he was, but that first battle had shown him it was impossible.

Another knock sounded at his door, this one lighter than Marshall's had been. What was it with everyone? Didn't they realise he wanted to be left alone? Unlocking it, he reefed the door open, about to demand what, when his sister threw herself into his arms.

"I just heard. Our father took Bellamy on patrol with him. How are-" she broke off as Marshall came to stand beside them. "You already know."

It was a statement, but Talon nodded anyway.

"I'm sorry."

Talon stepped back into his room, closing the door and gently pushing his sister from him. "There's nothing to be sorry about. I have my art."

"But-" she broke off with a glance at Marshall.

"She knows," Marshall accused.

"I haven't told her anything."

"She knows." Marshall stared at him, hurt in his eyes.

"I didn't tell her anything."

"Forget it." Marshall turned away, reaching for the door.

"Marshall-" he broke off. This was what he wanted. But why did he feel as bad as he'd felt the day he quit the army?

Marshall turned back to him, hope in his eyes.

He hesitated, but he had to kill that hope. "I'm sorry. I didn't want anyone to know. Not you, not my parents and especially not Garnet." His sister took his hand and squeezed tightly.

Marshall's gaze dropped to their hands, then met Talon's gaze again. "I would never betray you."

"I'm protecting you, not myself."

Marshall swore at him as he flung the door open and strode away.

Talon watched him go, his sister's hand still in his.

"I'm sorry." Garnet's words were whisper soft.

"It wasn't your fault."

"Yes, I-"

"It wasn't your fault." Talon let go of her hand to reach out and close the door, locking it before he strode to the window to watch the unit in the distance. He gripped the side frame of the window as his sister joined him. Anger rushed through him and he felt his back tighten. He barely managed to pull his shirt off before his wings burst forth. Would he ever be able to control the infernal things? He thought of the dagger in his boot. Another day. He'd try again another day.

Chapter Seven

Brianne

Brianne moaned, her hand reaching for the pain that made her head feel like it was on fire. A hand grabbed hold of hers before she could touch the wound.

"You'll be fine, soldier."

She dragged her eyes open to stare at the man who leaned over her, dark brown eyes meeting her gaze. "Where am I?" She tried to sit up and gratefully accepted the man's help. She looked around. It was late afternoon. She would have only been unconscious for several hours. Soldiers gathered dead bodies while some stood on guard, their gazes trained on the sky.

"You're a couple of hours from the capital. The Caelians have already collected their dead, you're lucky they didn't realise you were still alive."

She reached up to her head, her hand coming away bloodstained. When she saw Macklyn again, she had a score to settle.

"Name and rank soldier."

Brianne frowned, wincing at the pain that caused. "I don't know. I don't know anything." She tried to sound panicked.

"Take it easy, soldier. What's the last thing you recall?"

"Can you do me a favour?"

"What favour?"

Brianne shook her head and winced again. Macklyn would definitely pay for that. "No, that's the last thing I recall. Someone asking me that, but I can't see their face, it's all hazy." She hoped that was enough to lay the groundwork for when they started to try and discover who she was.

The man rose to his feet. "Over here, Bellamy."

"Yes, sir."

"You're in charge of this soldier. Get her back to the capital and to the hospital. Take one of the men with you. We'll be at your heels the moment we've gathered the dead."

"Yes, sir." He saluted before he turned to Brianne and held out his hand.

She hesitated, looking up into light brown eyes.

The young man had hair longer than hers, a dark brown that looked foreign to her after a lifetime of seeing blond hair and pale skin. Reaching up to take his hand, she noticed her skin was several shades paler than his dusky brown. She hoped she was dark enough not to make him question her. He pulled her to her feet before letting go of her hand.

"None of your unit's horses are here, you'll have to ride with me."

Brianne nodded and followed him to his horse. Once he was mounted, he swung her up behind him. "Who was that?" As they rode away, she gestured towards the man who'd first spoken to her.

"General Barrett Morin. I'm Bellamy Allard, unit captain." He slowed his horse as he passed one of the men. "Mount up, soldier. I need a guard for the journey back to the capital."

A general. Brianne wondered how she could use that to her advantage.

By the time Brianne reached the fortified capital, she couldn't have cared less who had found her. She wanted off the horse and wanted something to kill the pain in her head. Part of the ride had been spent imagining what she was going to do to Macklyn next time she saw him.

Bellamy dropped her at the hospital where she was

thoroughly examined before her head was cleaned and dressed. She was then shown to a bed in the ward where she drifted off to sleep, each noise drawing her awake. Hours later she was woken by a shadow falling across her and she opened her eyes to find Barrett standing there. He pulled a wooden, straight-backed chair up to her narrow bed and sat down.

"How are you feeling?"

"Like my head might explode. Other than that, I'm fine. I'm ready to get back to protecting our country, sir."

"Do you remember your name?"

"No sir, but I'm sure it'll come back to me soon." She eyed his broad shoulders, trying to get accustomed to how foreign everyone looked.

Barrett nodded. "We'll figure out who you are within the week. We're waiting for confirmation of which units haven't returned. A pity those cursed birds started taking identity tags a couple of months ago."

Brianne barely managed to keep her expression neutral. How long had they been planning to use her as a spy? And why had they waited until she'd received her ultimatum to tell her? "Thank you, sir."

Barrett rose to his feet. "Get some rest. The doctor said you should be ready to leave tomorrow."

"Where will I go, sir?"

"Don't worry about it, soldier. We won't leave you out in the rain." He spun on his heel and strode away.

Brianne stared after him, wondering how she was going to find useful information. She was still trying to figure it out when she drifted off to sleep. The next morning, she was woken early by a doctor who wanted to examine her.

The doctor pronounced her fit enough to leave. She donned yesterday's garments, which were now freshly laundered. There were dark stains on them and she wondered if it was from her blood or from the previous owner. Pushing that thought from her mind she headed towards the nearest exit. After asking for directions to the fortress, she wound her way through the city, her gaze darting everywhere. The streets were crowded with people and horses. She tried not to wrinkle her nose at the stench of manure left lying in the steadily warming day. How did they tolerate it? Stuck on the ground, never knowing the freedom of the skies.

She had to stop twice to ask for more directions to the fortress. When she reached it, she paused at the front to stare up at the imposing building. How was she meant to infiltrate that? She didn't have a clue, but standing outside wasn't going to get the job done. Marching inside, she was quickly halted by two soldiers.

"State your business."

"I'd like to see General Barrett Morin."

"Is the General expecting you?"

Brianne shook her head. "I want to thank him for rescuing me yesterday."

The same soldier spoke again. "We'll relay your thanks if you wish to leave a name."

She couldn't exactly do that. "Maybe I could wait here and see him when he has a moment." Laughter had her spinning to see a teenage girl with long black hair and golden brown skin staring at her out of brown eyes. She was starting to become accustomed to the dark colouring of the Tersten people.

"He doesn't have time for his own kids, I doubt he'll have time for you."

Brianne frowned as she tried to figure out how to use the situation to her advantage. "Have I met you before? Do you know me?"

"No, I've never seen you before."

"Oh. I had hoped... it's just that-" she cut off, turning away slightly. "It doesn't matter. I guess someone will figure out who I am eventually."

"You don't know who you are?" The girl looked up at her with wide eyes.

"I don't even know my first name. What's yours?"

"Garnet. How do you know my father? The General."

"He rescued me yesterday. I woke to find him leaning over me. It's the only real memory I have." She touched her bandaged head. "The doctors think the blow to my head made me forget everything."

"Wow. Then why are you here? Why aren't you still at the hospital?"

Before Brianne could answer, the soldier who'd spoken earlier interrupted. "Miss Morin, your father might prefer that you don't talk to strangers." He sent Brianne a hard look.

"You're right. I'm sorry. It's just that when I looked at Garnet I nearly caught hold of a memory. I hoped that meant she knew me. She must have reminded me of someone. Maybe a younger sister." Brianne took a step back. "I'm sorry to have bothered you. I guess I'll go…" her voice trailed away as she looked over her shoulder to the door. "Uhm, I don't know, somewhere." She turned and walked slowly away. With each footstep she mentally pleaded with Garnet to follow. She lowered her head, staring at the ground, letting her shoulders slump. Come on, kid. Stepping outside she kept her dejected pose as she walked forward. She'd nearly given up when the sound of running footsteps drew her attention.

"Wait." Garnet fell in beside her. "Where are you going?"

"I don't know." She looked around. The city was filled mostly with single and two storey buildings. Not one tower was in sight. "Nothing looks familiar. It's like I woke up in a foreign world yesterday, surrounded by the dead and drenched in blood."

"Really?"

Brianne nodded, hoping she hadn't painted too graphic a picture. "I don't even have any money for food and even if I did, I wouldn't have a clue where to buy it."

"You're hungry?"

Brianne stopped and looked at the young girl's eager face, a twinge of guilt hitting her. She nearly walked away, nearly ended the farce, but she forced herself to remember her people. All those who'd died and all those who risked death every day to defend her country. "Starving." She grinned. "I can't remember the last meal I ate." She couldn't count the light snack the hospital had given her last night as a meal.

Garnet laughed. "Come on. I'll buy you something

to eat. At least then you'll have one memory." She grabbed hold of Brianne's hand.

She allowed herself to be tugged along the street. "Better make it a large meal, I feel like I haven't eaten in a decade."

Chapter Eight

Talon

Talon stared at the summons from his father. It had been over a week since he'd seen him, let alone heard from him. He looked at the boy who'd cornered him in one of the corridors. "What does he want?"

The boy shrugged.

Talon stared at the kid, wondering if he'd overheard anything or really didn't know. "Tell him I'll be there later." He handed the piece of paper back to the boy.

"Sir, he said it was urgent. Said I had to find you quick."

"Tell him you found me, but tell him I'll be there later." Talon started to walk away.

"I don't know what it was about, just that he was yelling about your sister."

Talon froze, then spun to face the boy. "What about my sister?" Garnet's expression when she'd seen his wings came to mind.

He shrugged. "Don't know, sir. He was muttering and threatening then he tore up a letter and threw it in the rubbish and wrote that summons for you."

Talon stared at the boy who continued to meet his gaze. He nodded once. "I'll be there in a minute." Without waiting to hear another word he strode to his room. There was no way he could face his father without stretching his wings first.

Once the painful process was over, he hurried to his father's office and knocked on the door.

"Enter."

Talon stepped inside to find his father alone, seated at his desk with a scowl on his face.

"About time. I sent that boy for you ages ago."

"I was in the middle of something. What did you want?"

"For you to make yourself useful. Your infernal sister brought home a stray. Take care of her and find out all you can about her."

"Stray?"

"A soldier we found yesterday. Supposedly has no memory due to a blow to her head. Sit down Talon and stop towering over me."

Talon remained standing. "Why me?"

"Because Garnet refuses to give her up. You need to talk some sense into her. The woman could be dangerous."

That was his father. Everyone was guilty until they were proven innocent. "What am I meant to do with her?"

Barrett narrowed his eyes. "How about using that brain you prefer to let rot while you waste your days finger painting?"

His hands curled into fists and he breathed in slowly as he tried to rein in his anger. Why did his father always have to go on about his painting? "Where is she?"

"With Garnet. In my home."

"I'll see what I can do." Talon spun on his heel, striding from the office, slamming the door behind him.

"Stop slamming the infernal door," Barrett yelled after him.

Talon smiled fleetingly as he continued towards his father's apartment. Opening the front door, he paused in the foyer at the laughter that came through the doorway that led to the bedrooms. He stepped through and headed down the corridor to Garnet's room, stopping in the doorway to stare at the young woman laughing with his sister who was trying to show her a dance step.

Her hair was as short as his own, but seemed to be several shades lighter, as was her pale brown skin. She turned in his direction and he stared into pale brown eyes that quickly lost their laughter.

Garnet ran across the room to throw herself at him. "Talon." She drew away from him, grabbing his hands and pulling him into the room. "You show her. You know the steps so much better than I do."

Talon shook his head, drawing his hands from her. He studied the young woman who stared back at him. "I'm Talon." He held out his hand.

Garnet grinned when the woman took his hand. "This is Lacey. Don't you think she looks like a Lacey?"

Still holding the woman's hand, Talon turned to Garnet. "You named her?"

Garnet nodded.

"You can't go around naming people, Garnet."

Garnet shrugged, her chin rising. "She didn't have one, now she does."

Lacey drew her hand from his grip. "It's fine. I don't mind. It's a lovely name." She smiled at Garnet.

Talon felt his back tighten. He almost swore. Not

now. "Has Garnet showed you around? Found you somewhere to sleep?"

"She can stay in my room," Garnet said.

"I'm sure she'd rather have her own space," Talon said.

Garnet's eyes narrowed. "Did our father send you?"

Talon was tempted to tell her how much like their father she looked when she did that, but guessed now wasn't the time to point it out. "When have I ever been his lackey?"

"Then why are you here?" Garnet's hands went to her hips, her eyes still narrowed.

"To help." To protect you, but she wouldn't want to hear that.

"To help me or our father?"

Talon grinned. She was certainly her father's daughter. "Anyone ever tell you that sometimes you're overly suspicious?" He shot a glance towards Lacey. "But not enough at other times."

"I don't want to be any bother, Garnet. I'm sure I can find somewhere else to stay so you don't upset your father."

"Where will you stay?" Garnet demanded.

Lacey shrugged. "I don't know. There must be somewhere. After all you've done for me I'd hate to repay it by getting you in trouble."

Talon watched Lacey, wondering if it was all a performance or if she was exactly who she seemed to be. He turned to his sister. "I'll put her in the room next to mine. She'll only be several doors away from you. That'll keep our father happy, kind of, and you'll still be able to visit with her."

"You're not just saying that? You won't kick her out the next day? She doesn't know who she is. Doesn't know if she has a sister like me, if her parents are still alive, or anything. Her memories are completely gone."

So that was how she'd conned his sister. Or appealed to her. He still wasn't certain which one it was and he had to deal with it quickly before the pain from his wings drove him mad. "You can come with her, help her figure out what she needs for her room. Leave a note for our mother first or our father will be the least of your problems."

Garnet grinned and threw herself at him, holding him tightly. "I knew you wouldn't let me down. Just like I won't let you down."

Her hands brushed across his upper back and he gritted his teeth at the pain. "Go leave your note and we'll meet you at the room."

Garnet nodded and dashed from her bedroom.

Talon turned to Lacey. "I'll show you your new room." It was all he could do not to snarl the words.

Lacey followed him down the corridor towards the front door. "I'm sorry to be a problem. You can't imagine what it's like not knowing who you are."

"You'd be surprised at how well I can understand that."

"You've lost your memory before?"

He heard the surprise in her voice. "No." He didn't bother to explain and he was glad she didn't ask. He stopped in front of a door, flinging it open. He pointed to the door they'd passed. "I'm in there if you need me." He hurried away before she could speak and delay him. He was desperate to stretch his wings.

Chapter Nine

Brianne stared after Talon, wondering why he'd raced away. He wasn't what she'd expected from Garnet's comments. She mentally shrugged and turned towards the open doorway of the room she'd gained. It was better than being under Garnet's watchful eye. Hopefully she'd be able to do some exploring on her own. There had to be useful information somewhere in this place. After a glance up and down the empty corridor, she stepped into the room and closed the door.

The room was spacious, a narrow window in the wall directly across from the door, a large bed to the right of the door and a trunk at the foot of it. Off to her left was a small round table with two chairs and another trunk against the wall near them. A quick search showed no hidden places from where anyone could spy on her. The walls were solid stone, as was the floor, a woven rug on each side of the bed. A light blanket covered the bed and she hoped there'd be something thicker as the room felt cool now and it was barely the middle of the day.

Her inspection done, she turned back to the door and opened it to peer along the corridor. It was still empty. She wondered what had happened to Garnet. Closing the door behind her, she headed for Talon's room. Maybe he'd taken Garnet aside while she'd been busy exploring her room. If she lost Garnet's support she'd probably be out of the fortress and lose any chance to gather useful information.

She knocked on the timber door and waited. No one answered. Where was he? Had he gone back to the General's home? She looked along the corridor then knocked one last time.

"What?"

She eyed the door, uncertain if she should continue to disturb Talon after the way he'd snarled. "Talon?" There was silence. She nearly gave up when the door opened.

"What?"

His shirt was half buttoned, sweat dotted his upper

lip and he seemed a little pale under the golden brown tone of his skin. "Are you well?"

"What do you want?"

She nearly walked away until she saw how he gripped the door, his knuckles white. Reaching out to touch his cheek with the back of her hand she asked again, "Are you well?"

He stepped away, grabbing her hand before she could make contact. "What do you want?"

Brianne met his gaze, recognising the pain in his eyes. She'd seen it in her own many times after she'd turned eighteen and her wings hadn't developed. She resisted the urge to touch her shoulder blades. "I was wondering where Garnet is." Pulling away from him, she glanced around, her gaze arrowing in on a large black feather on the floor several feet from her. She was across the room, Talon at her heels, grabbing her wrist as her fingers seized the feather.

"What are you doing?" Talon demanded.

Rising to her feet, she tried to pull from his grip, but it tightened. "Where did you get this?" She held his gaze, the feather feeling so familiar in her hands. The size, the shape, the feel. Only the colour was different.

"Where is she?"

They both turned to face Garnet who had burst into the room.

Garnet's gaze was drawn first to Brianne and then to Talon. "Oh, sorry. It's just that our father came home and asked if you'd got rid of Lacey yet. I thought-" She stopped abruptly, her gaze falling to their hands. "Oh." Her hands rose, pressing against her mouth.

Talon shook his head. "No, Garnet."

Brianne looked from one to the other. It wasn't possible, was it? "Where did this come from?"

"I found it," Garnet blurted out. She pointed towards the window. "Out there. Past the city walls when I was out riding on my own. I wasn't meant to be there on my own. Please don't tell anyone."

Brianne tugged her hand away from Talon. This time he let her go. "Did you see what it came from?"

Garnet shook her head, her gaze sliding to Talon and then back again.

"Are you sure?" Brianne ran a finger along the feather, her gaze still on Garnet.

Garnet nodded, another glance at Talon.

There was definitely something she wasn't saying and Brianne was determined to find out, but she knew that sometimes retreat was the best strategy. She smiled slightly. "Can I keep it, please? It's so beautiful. I only wish I knew what sort of creature it came from. It must be majestic." Her gaze was drawn to the feather and she ran a finger down the centre of it. Her voice dropped. "Beautiful." How she wished she owned wings of her own, filled with feathers like these. Even black wings would be better than no wings. Although knowing her people they'd probably still think her an abomination. Wings were meant to be white. A sound from Talon drew her gaze. She stared at him, trying to figure out what his expression meant.

"Keep it, but get out. I was in the middle of painting." His voice was harsh.

"You paint?" She couldn't keep the surprise from her voice.

"He paints all the time. He hates being disturbed when he's creating a masterpiece," Garnet said.

She didn't believe them. "Maybe I can have a look at it when it's finished."

"I'll never get it finished if people don't stop annoying me," Talon growled.

"Do you want me to help you figure out what you need for your room?" Garnet asked. "Guest rooms are very boring and very basic so you're sure to need something."

Brianne nodded, not wanting to alienate her only

ally. "A thicker blanket would be good." She followed Garnet from the room, glancing over her shoulder at Talon who remained motionless, as if movement was too painful. Closing the door behind her, she let Garnet's chatter wash over her.

She had to figure out what they were hiding. Was one of her people captive here? But why a black feather? Maybe that's what vieteh berries did to feathers. Although surely not. Wouldn't she have seen someone with black wings before now if that was the case? She didn't have a clue, but she was going to find out. Somehow.

Chapter Ten

Talon

Talon still felt tired. He'd tossed and turned all night. His wings had woken him. He'd tried to keep them retracted, but it had been impossible. While he'd lain awake in pain, he'd thought of Lacey and the way she'd caressed his feather. Majestic. What did she know? She didn't have to live with them.

Standing in the empty corridor, he knocked on Lacey's door for the second time, louder than before. She didn't answer. He tried the door and it swung open. The room was empty. Where was she? After a quick look in the two trunks and finding nothing out of the ordinary, he headed off to search for her. He didn't get far before he was stopped by a boy holding out what he guessed was a summons from his father.

"What does he want now?"

The boy took a hurried step back at his tone, the folded paper still held out.

Talon sighed heavily and took the paper, glancing over it before he shoved it back at the boy. What did his father want now? More strays for him to look after? What was wrong with Bellamy babysitting? Ignoring the boy who trotted at his side, Talon strode towards his father's office. Annoyed by his constant demands, he didn't bother knocking. The boy stayed in the corridor, obviously smarter than he looked.

"What do you want now?"

Barrett looked up from his paperwork. "If you had bothered to join us for the morning meal you'd already know."

His jaw clenched and his back tightened as he thought of his morning. Kneeling on the cold floor, head thrown back as pain racked his body, wings outstretched after being retracted part of the night. His sleep was always broken, fear bringing him awake regularly, the bandages preventing his wings from spreading out in his sleep until pain forced him to set them free.

"What do you want?"

"What have you learned about the girl?"

He should have known his father would expect a report. "Nothing."

"Why not?"

"I was busy separating her from Garnet. Wasn't that the main priority?"

"Then you didn't do a very good job, she complained all morning about going with her mother. Said she'd made plans to spend the day with the stray. Looney or whatever she calls her."

"Lacey."

"Find out who she is. Ask her questions. Watch what she does. Where is she right now?"

His back tightened as his hands became fists. "How in the Infernal World would I know? I can't be in two places at once."

"Then get out there and find her if you've nothing useful to tell me." Barrett made a sharp gesture towards the door.

Talon glared at his father a moment longer before he spun on his heel and marched from the room, slamming the door behind him. He couldn't even dredge up a smile as his father's curses rang out behind him.

It took him nearly an hour to find Lacey and when she saw him, there was a moment of fear before she walked towards him with a smile.

"Thank the Lord and Lady. I'm so lost I haven't a clue where I am." Her expression froze.

"Did you remember something?"

"No, I mean, yes, but-" she made a vague gesture with her hand.

"Maybe I should take you to the House of the Lord and Lady since they seem to have something to do with your memory."

"The House..." her words trailed away.

He tried to interpret her expression. "Yes, do you remember something about it?"

She shook her head. "No, but something about it sounds familiar. Could you take me there?"

Talon wanted to say no, but his father had ordered him to watch her. He didn't know how he was expected to do that with the amount of time he spent in his room every day. His back tightened slightly and he wondered if he should make an excuse so he could stretch his wings before he took her there. Surely he'd be fine for a while. It wasn't that long since he'd stretched them. "Just a quick visit."

"Thank you. You can't imagine how much it means to me that you and your sister are willing to help me try and regain my memories."

Feeling uncomfortable at her praise, he gave her a curt nod before he silently led the way through the corridors. Once outside, he increased his pace as they headed down the street.

"Lacey!"

Talon turned at the shout and scowled at the sight of Bellamy across the street waving at her.

She stopped with a smile, returning the wave.

Talon fought to keep his wings retracted. "Are we going to the House? I don't have all day to show you around." He fell silent as Bellamy drew closer.

Lacey turned to Talon, her smile still in place. "Only a moment. I want to thank him for bringing me back. I was in so much pain I don't think I remembered to."

Bellamy reached them before Talon could reply. His grin became a sneer as he turned towards Talon, a nod in his direction. "Talon."

"Bellamy." He bit the word out, not even bothering with a polite nod.

"How are you faring, Lacey?" The curt tone left Bellamy's voice.

When Lacey smiled up at Bellamy, Talon felt his anger and pain increase. "How do you know her name?" His hand ached for the sword he'd stopped wearing the day he'd quit the army.

"Garnet told me this morning."

"What were you doing talking to Garnet?" Bellamy had no business being around his sister.

Bellamy's smile remained in place, becoming a

touch insolent. "She was with the General this morning when I was receiving new orders."

Lacey took a step forward, her shoulder separating them as she reached out to clasp Bellamy's hand. "I wanted to thank you for rescuing me."

"It was a pleasure."

"I'll say a prayer for you while I'm at the House of the Lord and Lady."

"You're going there now?" Bellamy glanced up the road in the direction they'd been travelling. "I have some time spare if you'd like company."

Talon nearly growled. Bellamy always had to push in and take what wasn't his. "She already has company." He grabbed Lacey's hand, fighting against the pain as he strode up the street, pulling Lacey with him.

Chapter Eleven

Brianne

Brianne tugged her hand from Talon's grip, annoyed he'd chased Bellamy away. How was she meant to find useful information if he kept getting in the way? Did he suspect something? Had that been why he'd come looking for her? She had to be more careful, he'd nearly caught her entering a door she'd had no business opening. While exploring, she'd watched a boy take a stack of papers from the General's office and drop them in the room Talon had found her near. She'd search it later. There might be important information in some of those papers.

For now she'd make do with learning where different areas were. "Can you slow down? This pace is making my head ache." It wasn't effecting the dull ache she'd had all day, but hopefully her comment would make him feel guilty enough to walk slower so she could check the area.

Talon slowed. "It's not bandaged anymore."

"That doesn't mean it's stopped aching." He seemed a little more sympathetic and was now walking slow enough so she could take in more of her surroundings.

"Do you remember anything from before your injury?" Talon gestured towards her head.

"No. My dreams last night were filled with vague images, but nothing clear. All they did was disturb my sleep."

"I'm sorry."

She met his gaze, surprised to find not the sympathy she had expected, but understanding. She frowned. "Are you well?" He didn't look as bad as he had yesterday, but it looked like he wasn't far off it.

"Why do you keep asking me that? I'm fine. Come on, I haven't got all day."

Brianne glared at his back as he strode ahead of her. That was the last time she'd bother. Not if he was going to act like that. Looking past him, her mouth dropped open and she stared at the House of the Lord and Lady, the building so familiar she might as well have been at home. Closing her mouth, she glanced around to make sure no one had noticed her standing there like an idiot. Ahead of her, Talon stopped and turned to face her, his arms crossing his chest when he spotted her. She hurried forward.

"Do you remember it?" Talon demanded as she reached him.

It took her long moments to figure out an answer as she met his gaze. "It feels very familiar." She walked towards the entrance, pausing in the doorway. "Very familiar." Her words were softer this time.

Beneath her feet the dark polished timber floor was streaked with colour from the stained glass windows. Her gaze was drawn upwards to see the familiar robed figures with hands cupped and raised in supplication in the stained glass. Ahead of her was the altar, white marble draped in a white silk cloth. Several slow steps forward brought her to the pews. She reached out hesitantly, her fingers touching the honeyed tones of the fine-grained wood that had been worn by centuries of use. The only difference to the carved ends was that the figures had no wings.

She sat heavily in the closest pew before her knees gave out. Her mind swam as she tried to figure out what it meant. The only contact their two countries had had for the past several centuries was through weapons. How was it possible they worshipped the same gods and built the same buildings for them? What else was the same? And why?

Talon sat beside her, a wry smile twisting his lips. "Will you snarl at me if I ask you if you're well?"

Brianne smiled weakly. "Where is the earthly dwelling of the Master of the Infernal World?" She almost held her breath as she waited for his answer.

"In the southern most point of the city."

She fought to remain calm, clasping her hands together.

"Don't tell me you worship him. You're a soldier."

Shaking her head, she gripped her hands tighter when she noticed the tremble in them. "No. I'm trying to make sense of the jumble of words and images in my head." Tying to make sense of the entire situation. A sound from behind drew her attention and panic hit as she saw the reddish-brown robed penitent walking towards them. A quick glance around showed nowhere to hide. "I… I… my family…" She took deep gulps of air, as the penitent came closer. "I want to know who I am." She reached out for Talon, her hands grasping his shoulders as she pressed her head against his chest, her face turned away from the aisle.

After a moment, Talon patted her back. "I'm sure it'll all come back to you. Give it time."

Her face hidden, panic receded and Brianne realised that the robed penitent wouldn't be someone she knew. The facelessness of the hooded figure had reminded her so much of the ones from home she'd momentarily feared she was caught. But it was too late to change tactics now. "It's taking too long." She kept her face pressed against his chest, lowering her hands. One she rested near her face on his chest the other started to encircle him.

Talon pushed her away, grabbing her hand from his side. "I'll take you back to your room."

She was about to argue when she noticed he looked more unwell, sweat beading his upper lip and forehead, his jaw clenched tight. He reminded her of the old men who'd been injured in battle, particularly when a storm was due, and they fought against the pain from injuries the doctors had never been able to completely heal. "Are you injured?"

Rising to his feet, Talon shook his head, holding out his hand, remaining silent.

It was a moment before she took the offered hand and rose to her feet, the heat of his hand unnaturally warm. The journey back to her room was rushed and several times Talon's grip on her hand tightened, but she held back the questions she wanted to ask. When they reached her room he nearly pushed her into it, striding to his own and slamming the door behind him.

Stepping into the corridor, Brianne stared at his closed door. What was his problem? She took a deep breath to calm herself. It had been a long morning, but she still hadn't found anything useful. Maybe now was the time. She would return to the room she'd been about to enter when Talon had caught her earlier.

Chapter Twelve

Talon

Talon fought against the pain as he lay half curled on the stone floor of his room. He gasped as he held back the roar that hovered at the back of his throat. Lacey was next door. He couldn't make a sound. What stupid idea had possessed him to put her there? A drawn out groan escaped and he closed his eyes, trying to block out the pain. Eventually he was left panting on the floor, his wings retracting as he rolled onto his side. He wasn't going to survive much more of this. The pain seemed to be getting worse. How did those infernal birds cope?

He staggered to his feet and began the process of bandaging himself and getting out another shirt. Bundling up the one now missing buttons, he shoved it in the bottom of his trunk with the other ones he needed to fix. Soon he'd have none left.

Running a hand over the dark stubble on his head he took a deep breath and looked towards his door. He guessed it was time he returned to spying on Lacey. The memory of her hand sliding along his side headed for his back came to mind. It had been a long time since he'd made the mistake of letting someone get close enough to discover his secret. Garnet didn't count. She'd been in the wrong place and he'd been in too much pain to even think of checking his room.

He paused at his door, resting his head against the timber as he tried to convince himself he needed to keep an eye on Lacey. If it wasn't for her involvement with Garnet, he'd have told his father to find someone else to investigate her. An image of Lacey holding Bellamy's hand had him straightening his shoulders and marching to her room. Knocking brought no answer. He didn't bother knocking a second time, just opened the door. Like earlier, the room was empty.

Turning on his heel he strode through corridors, annoyed he had to once again look for her. He found her headed down the same corridor he'd caught her in last time. Trying to remain quiet so he could see what she was up to, he moved closer.

Lacey spun to face him, her hand going to her side as if she reached for a sword. Her wary expression relaxed and she smiled at him. "What were you doing sneaking up on me? You're lucky I didn't have a sword."

"What are you doing here again?"

"Again?" She frowned as she glanced around. "Oh, you're right. I thought it looked familiar, but I thought that was because I was headed for the main exit." She sighed. "I wonder if I've always had such a terrible sense of direction." Another smile. "Maybe I need a map."

The smile made his back tighten and he nearly cursed. Terrific. That was all he needed. Writhing on the ground in pain again. "Where were you going?"

Lacey shrugged. "Out. I don't know." She shrugged again. "I thought maybe something might look familiar if I explored a bit."

Talon stared at her, trying to decide if she spoke the truth. It was impossible to tell. Maybe he could follow her more successfully around the city. "I'll show you where the exit is and leave you to explore on your own. I have other things I need to do this afternoon."

"Like what?"

It took him a second to think. "Paint."

"Can I see what you're painting?"

"No." He remained silent as they strode through the corridors to the main exit. He stopped just outside, crossing his arms as he watched her.

"Thank you. I'm sorry I'm such a bother."

Talon shrugged.

"Will I see you tonight?"

Not if he could help it. "Why?"

"Garnet invited me to dinner."

Talon managed to hold back a smile at the thought of how his father would react when he found out. Now that would be worth leaving his room for. "I wouldn't miss it for the world."

Lacey nodded, looking from him to the city. "I guess I'll…" her words trailed off and she finished the sentence with a gesture towards the street.

Talon nodded.

Lacey stared at him a moment longer before she turned and hurried off into the street, matching her pace to the crowd as she walked along with it.

Talon had no trouble keeping her in sight. The problem was the lack of cover during the times she looked around, supposedly trying to find something familiar. Then he realised where she was leading them. Without hesitation she was following the exact path they'd taken to the House of the Lord and Lady, right down to the two shortcuts he preferred to use.

His eyes narrowed as he studied her. There was no way she'd been lost in the fortress, there had to be a reason she was in that corridor. The only one he could think of was the room of the officer who received all the paperwork that needed to be filed in the storerooms.

Did she know about that room? And how did she know? What was he going to tell his father? It was only a suspicion, nothing concrete, but instinct screamed he was right. What was her plan? What did she hope to gain from spying on his father?

He stayed back as he watched her circle around the House. Why didn't she go inside? Was she meeting with someone? Trailing behind her, he waited for her to give herself away. Instead, she stared up at stained glass windows, slowly moving around the building until she was at the front again. The only entrance. What in the name of the Lord and Lady was she up to? He rubbed at his shoulder blade, trying to ease the tightness, wishing he could remove the bandage and set his wings free before they became painful.

Chapter Thirteen

Brianne

There was only one entrance. Brianne frowned. Just like at home. One path to the Lord and Lady. And if everything else was the same, then maybe they had history archives too. It was worth a try.

Taking a hesitant step forward, Brianne forced herself to straighten her shoulders and take the next step with more confidence. She might need to ask something of them, but that didn't mean she had to go shuffling forth with head bowed and begging.

Looking around at the inside of the almost familiar building, she saw a penitent, not far from the altar, replacing burnt out candles with fresh ones. Striding forward, she kept her gaze mostly on the penitent, with an occasional glance around to check her surroundings. She was nearly upon the penitent before they looked up, the hood creating dark shadows where a face should be.

"Welcome to the House of the Lord and Lady, how may I serve you?" A masculine voice came from the hooded figure.

Her stomach lurched. She was about to lie to a servant of the gods. She really hoped that when she had to face the reckoning at the end of her life they'd accept that it was for a good cause. "Holy One, I suffered a head injury recently while I was on patrol and lost the memories of my entire past."

"I am sorry for your suffering. Would you like me to pray for you?"

"No, well yes. But I also wondered if you could help me with something else. I know nothing. Not only is my history gone, but that of our people. The Lord and Lady are names, the Master of the After World also an unknown deity. I thought if I could read our history and learn it all over again it might help bring back some of my memories." She hated how she couldn't see the penitent's features. How could she tell if her words were having the effect she wanted? Even the hands were covered by gloves. She'd never thought about it before. Summer must be unbearable for them covered up like this. All of them. The Supreme One, Elders and the penitents.

"I am sorry, I wish I could help. No one can enter the archives without first gaining permission from the Supreme One. He is the only one who has the key, but he is currently away communing with the gods."

She barely masked her disappointment. "Do you know when he'll be back?"

"When the gods have told him all they wish him to hear."

Brianne nodded, the words so very familiar. The Supreme One for her people came and went according to the dictates of the Lord and Lady too. "I'll come again another day. If you might pray for me in the meantime, Holy One?"

"I would be honoured." The head dipped and the hands were momentarily raised in supplication.

"Thank you." Brianne turned away, trying to walk softly through the otherwise quiet building. She would have to come up with another plan. Maybe things would be different at the earthly dwelling of the Master of the Infernal World. Stepping outside, she raised her gaze to the sky, checking for the location of the sun. It was strange to look into the sky and see no towers reaching skywards, no winged people travelling from building to building, sometimes hovering as they greeted a friend. The skies here were empty.

Once she'd figured out the direction the Master's dwelling should be in, she wound her way through streets. As she drew near to the wall around the city, knowing she must be close, she asked a passerby for directions. She had less luck in the Master's dwelling. They directed her to the Supreme One, telling her only the House of the Lord and Lady kept the archives.

Feeling like the day had been wasted, Brianne headed to the fortress only to be stopped at the entrance. "I'm staying here." Her tone was polite, none of her annoyance leaking through.

"I've had no word of anyone new living at the fortress," the soldier said.

He was a different soldier to the first one Brianne had met, but seemed to be equally as difficult. "I'm staying with the General and his family."

"No one has informed me. If you have no proof, I can't let you in."

How was she meant to get proof? "Send for one of them. Any of the General's family could tell you I'm staying here."

"I'm sorry, but I can't disturb the General unless it's an emergency."

Brianne glared at him, his arrogant tone increasing her annoyance. "Then have someone fetch Garnet."

"I can't have the General's daughter brought before someone who might be a stranger and a risk to her."

A scream of frustration stirred inside her. "Then fetch Talon."

The soldier shook his head. "I'm afraid you'll have to find some other way to prove you're meant to be here. Now please move on and stop causing trouble."

There was no other way she could prove she was meant to be there. It was impossible. Frustration filled her and she stepped away, staring into the city as she tried to figure out what to do. Would Garnet wonder where she was when she didn't turn up to dinner? A glance over her shoulder showed the soldier still watched her. Was this normal behaviour or had the General ordered them not to let her back in if she returned alone. She needed to get into the fortress. How could she return to her people with nothing to help them? She couldn't. Taking another couple of steps forward, her gaze searched the area. There were no answers.

No way in and nowhere else to go. Her right hand curled at her side, wishing she had her sword. Then she'd have shown the guard what she thought of his attitude. Him and his fellow guard. No one had been able to beat her in any of her classes. She sighed.

None of her training had helped. She rubbed at her shoulder. Not one single bit.

"Why are you standing here?"

Brianne turned to see Talon. He'd snuck up on her while she'd been busy wallowing in self-pity and she hadn't noticed. She had to be more careful. "They won't let me in." She glanced towards the soldiers guarding the main entrance.

"Why?"

"Apparently I have no proof I'm staying here and they wouldn't fetch anyone who could vouch for me." Talon remained quiet long enough that she began to think he mightn't be willing to vouch for her.

Then he nodded and held out his hand. "Come on."

She took the hand with a grateful smile. "Thank you."

"I haven't got you inside yet. Maybe he's decided neither of us are welcome back."

Brianne didn't need to ask who 'he' was. She walked beside Talon, unable to resist giving the soldier a smile as she stepped into the building. It looked like it was only her who wasn't welcome.

Chapter Fourteen

Talon

Pushing the food around on his plate, Talon made a pretence of eating. The pain had been steadily increasing and he didn't think the food would stay down if he ate it. He was tempted to rise from the table and leave. It couldn't make his father any angrier with him. The meal seemed like it would last forever and everything Lacey had said about what she'd done that afternoon had sounded so plausible. Maybe too plausible. He didn't know what to think.

Garnet was telling their mother something and Talon couldn't focus enough to work out what she was saying. He'd had enough. Rising to his feet, he pushed away from the table.

"Where are you going?" Barrett demanded.

"Out."

"You haven't finished eating." Barrett pointed towards the barely touched plate with his knife.

He started to reply, but a wave of pain had him clenching his teeth and he turned away from the table.

"Talon!"

Ignoring the roar of his father, Talon stumbled away. Then he was in his room, locking the door and uncertain of how he'd made it there. His fingers trembled as he tried to undo the buttons of his shirt. He lost only one this time and threw the shirt in a heap on the ground, the bandages joining it as his wings sprung free. Throwing his head back he opened his mouth as if to scream, but held the sound in. Falling to the ground, his hands and knees drew in the cold of the floor, but it didn't reduce the heat that raged through him.

As soon as he was past the worst of the pain he staggered to his feet. Taking his sword from under his bed where he stored it, he pulled it free from the scabbard. He slashed at the canvas he'd started, to replace the one he'd burned. It was an improvement. A knock at the door had him spinning to stare at it, sword still raised, wings cloaking him.

"Talon?"

"Go away, Lacey."

"Are you well?"

He groaned, lowering the sword. Why had she followed him? Couldn't they all leave him alone?

"Talon?"

Not bothering to answer, he focused on retracting his wings. Resting his sword against his legs, he pulled on his shirt to hide the ridges on his back, doing up the buttons with shaky hands.

"Talon?" She knocked lightly on the door.

Not bothering to put away his sword, he ripped the door open. "What?"

Lacey stared up at him for several moments before she smiled. "You planning to use that against me?" She nodded towards the sword.

"I never attack an unarmed person."

"I'm not unarmed. I have a dagger in my boot." The smile remained in place.

Talon relaxed a little. "That hardly seems fair. I'll wait until you have a sword."

"I'm willing to make do with the dagger. I miss training every day." Her eyes rounded and her smile was replaced by a gasp as she covered her mouth with her hand.

"Your memory's back?"

She shook her head. "No, but I remembered something." Her horrified expression was replaced by a grin. "I actually remembered something. Maybe it's starting to come back." She frowned. "I can't think of anything else though."

Talon continued to watch her, trying to figure her out. She was either telling the truth or a really good actress. There was one thing he could test. "Tomorrow."

"What?"

"I'll organise a sword for you to use tomorrow. We can practice in here." He gestured behind him. "It's more than big enough." He was surprised by the look of excitement that entered her eyes.

"Really?" At his nod, her grin returned. "I can't wait." She started to turn away then faced him again. "Are you certain you're well?"

Talon ignored the question. "I'll see you in the morning."

"They argued about you when you left."

"They argue about me when I'm there too."

Her expression was serious as she stared silently at him. Then her smile returned. "You might want to wear armour. I plan to win, whatever it takes."

"I'll see if I can find some armour in your size. I never lose."

She grinned and with a nod, sauntered back to her

room, glancing his way before she entered and closed the door behind her.

Talon continued to stand in the corridor a moment longer before he closed his own door, surprised to find he was actually smiling. She better be as good as she said. It had been far too long since he'd had someone to practice against and he could hardly wait for morning to arrive.

Chapter Fifteen

Brianne

The next morning, Brianne parried an attack, adrenaline coursing through her. "Is that the best you can do? You're not even trying." She had woken at daybreak and it had taken all her willpower not to knock on Talon's door and demand they start immediately.

Talon smiled lazily, his attack not much more energetic. "I wouldn't want to wear you out in the first quarter hour."

"Are you sure? I'd have thought you'd want to get this over and done with and return to your masterpiece you keep telling me about." She grinned, wanting this training session to last for hours. This was her, not the spy skulking around corners looking for obscure information.

"There's plenty of time. Are you worried you'll tire easily?"

"I could have disarmed you a dozen times already, but I was worried I'd damage your ego."

Talon laughed. "You're dreaming. I could deal with you in my sleep."

"Keep telling yourself that." Brianne attacked, thinking that this was the person Garnet had told her about. She'd never seen him so alive. In the name of the Lord and Lady why had he ever quit the army? He was like her, born to be a fighter. A pity he was on the wrong side.

"I don't need to tell myself anything. My actions speak for me."

She laughed, joy filling the sound as she renewed her efforts. He was good, matching her blow for blow. The sound of metal rang out in the room, early morning light spilling in through the single window. If she'd had wings he wouldn't have stood a chance, as it was, she didn't know who'd win. But even without wings, she could almost fly. Leaping to the side, she spun around and came up on the other side of him, attacking. His blade barely came around in time to block. Then he was attacking her.

There was no time for laughter as she fought back, gliding out of the way, spinning, weaving, even using some of the acrobatic moves she'd learned in preparation for growing wings. He couldn't touch her. But she couldn't touch him either. Time trickled away, the daylight shifting across the floor. Then he nearly had her and she ducked and came up on the other side of him. He turned to try and meet her blade, but he was too slow and she caught him across the chest, blood instantly staining his shirt.

Jumping backwards, she lowered her sword. "I'm sorry. I thought you'd block that attack. Maybe we should have used armour."

He made a flicking motion with his free hand. "Barely a scratch. You're not giving in are you?"

"If you want to be shredded one scratch at a time I don't mind."

He gestured for her to come at him.

Adrenaline still coursing through her, she willingly obeyed, feeling more alive than she had in ages. Their breathing was heavy, their movements fast. Time was measured in the clang of metal. And then Talon stumbled and Brianne barely managed to pull back in time to avoid cutting him again. She reached for him.

He pulled away from her. "Keep going."

She didn't let him retreat. Her hand brushed against his cheek. "You've got a fever."

"I'm fine." He pushed her hand away.

"Have you seen a doctor?"

"Don't blame me if you're too exhausted to go on."

"I drew blood, you didn't. Don't try and tell me I've lost."

"It was the first to disarm, nothing was said about first blood."

"Talon-"

"Damn it, I can do this. Don't treat me like I'm sick."

She stepped back from the anger in his voice. "We'll call it a temporary draw. We can continue tomorrow morning." She took a wary step towards him. "Let me check your scratch."

He grabbed her hand before it could reach him. "It's fine."

Sheathing her sword in the scabbard she'd hung at her side she nodded. "You better not use it as an excuse tomorrow." She met his gaze, seeing pain in his eyes. Before he had a chance to react, she reached out with the hand that was still free and tugged at the neck of his shirt. He let her go, pulling away, but not before she saw the bandage wrapped around his chest. "You're injured."

"It's nothing."

Guilt hit her. "You fought me while you were already injured. Are you crazy? Is that why you quit the army? How bad is it? I didn't make it worse, did I?"

"Just go."

"Talon–"

"Go." He pointed towards the door.

About to argue, Brianne changed her mind when she saw the tremble in his hand. "This match isn't over." She stared at him a moment more before she spoke again. "Tomorrow morning." When he nodded, she strode to the door and left, closing it softly behind her. She stood there, trying to decide what to do and was still standing there when Talon locked the door. She heard a tortured groan and reached for the door.

Her hand curled into a fist, but dropped to her side before it met the door. He didn't want her in there. His ego probably couldn't cope with someone seeing him weak. Turning towards her own room, she shook her head at his stupidity. It all made so much sense now. No wonder he was often cranky and left abruptly. But it didn't help her mission any. Her people wouldn't care that the General's son had been injured in battle. She still had to find out something useful and she had no clue how to go about it. What had made them think she could complete this mission? She hoped it wasn't just her lack of wings because so far that hadn't done her much good.

At least she should be able to explore unhindered if Talon was going to hole up in his room. She thought of the room she'd tried to search several times now. Maybe this time she'd get lucky and see what was stored inside.

Chapter Sixteen

Talon

Talon paced the floor as he waited for Lacey to arrive for their second practice session. He'd been an idiot yesterday. He should have stopped sooner. It wasn't necessary that he win. After a moment he smiled wryly. Of course it was necessary, but he couldn't last that long without his wings wanting to escape their confines. He'd have to call a halt before he got to that stage today. It wasn't losing, what had Lacey called it? Temporary truce. He could live with that. Maybe.

But it had been so long since he'd had someone to train with. Even though he'd quit the army, he hadn't been able to convince himself to stop training. There was nothing like pitting your skills against an opponent and trying to win. But as much as he enjoyed training with her, he couldn't keep ignoring the fact that he kept finding her in areas she shouldn't be. If only he could find proof either way. He didn't want to tell his father when it was only a suspicion. His father would accept that as guilt without looking further.

A knock brought him to a sudden stop and he headed back to the door, swinging it open, his sword in a scabbard at his side. He tried not to return the smile Lacey wore when he looked down at her, but it was impossible. He wanted to drag her inside and demand they start straight away.

"Good morning."

Talon stepped aside and gestured her in. "What took you so long to get here? Did you have to build up your courage to face my superior skills?"

With a laugh, Lacey stepped inside. "You better be well today because I want you to know it was my superior skills that caused you to be disarmed. No blaming it on old injuries."

About to answer, his attention was caught by his father striding along the corridor towards his room. At a signal from his father, he waited, Lacey coming closer to stand at his shoulder. Uncomfortable with her at his back, he stepped further into the corridor, standing at an angle so he could see both his father and Lacey.

Barrett opened his mouth, snapping it closed as his gaze fell on Lacey in the doorway. "Have you regained your memory yet?"

She shook her head. "No, sir. Only a couple of vague memories that don't help at all."

His gaze was drawn to the sword at her side and he nodded towards it. "Where did you get that?"

Lacey continued to meet Barrett's gaze. "It's not mine, sir. I borrowed it so I can continue to train. As soon as the doctors declare me fit for duty I plan to be back on patrol, sir."

"Who does it belong to?" Barrett demanded.

When Lacey remained silent, Talon answered for her. "I'm working with her."

"You're training again?" Barrett demanded.

"No."

"Then what's going on?"

"I asked him to partner me while I train, sir."

Talon looked towards Lacey, surprised by her defence of him, before his gaze returned to his father. "Did you have a reason to be here at this time of day? Aren't you usually holed up in your office or tearing strips off soldiers on the training grounds by now?" He met his father's hard look, keeping his expression neutral when a stab of pain shot across his back.

Barrett eventually turned his attention to Lacey.

"We've narrowed your identity down to three people. Tomorrow morning the mother of one of those soldiers will be here to see you. I'll bring her to your room."

Talon watched Lacey carefully, like he was certain his father would be, but he couldn't be sure if the slight hesitation was panic or amazement. Then she grinned, her entire face lighting up as she clasped her hands at chest height.

"She can't get here any sooner? I don't know how I'm going to be able to wait that long. And what about the families of the other two soldiers? When do I see them? Tomorrow?"

Barrett nodded. "One in the afternoon, but I don't know when the third family will arrive. We haven't been able to get in touch with them yet."

"I hope it is my mother. I don't think I can wait days to find out. You can't imagine how difficult it is not knowing who you are." She turned to Talon, her grin still in place. "I don't know how I'm going to be able to concentrate to train."

"Are you getting your excuses ready for when you lose?"

Lacey laughed. "Just trying to match you excuse for excuse."

"What excuse have you got," Barrett demanded of Talon.

He answered before Lacey could mention his supposed injury. "Lack of practice."

"You only have yourself to blame for that. Wasting a god given talent is a sin."

Talon met his father's stare, refusing to back down. "It is, which is why I've chosen to focus on my painting."

Lacey took a step into the corridor, drawing both their attentions. "I'm sorry if having you train with me has been such a chore. I'll let you return to your painting if you prefer."

Talon shook his head. "It's fine." He turned to his father. "Was that all?" It better be. He wasn't having him chase away Lacey before he had a chance to train.

Barrett nodded, not bothering to speak before he turned on his heel and strode away. Talon stared after him until his attention was caught by Lacey moving back into the room.

A hint of a smile curved her lips. "Ready to be humiliated?"

Talon grinned, stepping into the room to lock the door behind him. "I think you're talking about the wrong person." He drew his sword. "You have an hour to try and disarm me, but if yesterday is any indication, you're going to fail." Surely he could manage an hour without his wings interfering.

"Fail?" Lacey laughed. "And who was the one bleeding yesterday?" She leapt forward, swinging her sword as she spun away.

Talon continued to grin, feeling alive as he fought her. She seemed half bird as she flew around the room. If he knew how to use his infernal wings he'd show her what it meant to fly. His back tightened and he forced himself to focus on keeping them retracted. But they wanted to break free, wanted to help him soar around the room like Lacey seemed to be able to do without any wings. "This is a fight, not a dance. I don't think Garnet needed to show you any dance moves, you have more than enough of your own."

"You poor thing. Do you need your opponent to stay still before you can defeat them? It's not my fault if you're too slow to keep up."

"Slow?" He attacked rapidly, as she kept up her impression of a bird, darting in and out. "You better look out because I'm about to clip your wings and you won't be flying around the room anymore." A strange expression crossed Lacey's face and she faltered. He nearly cut her and barely managed to draw back in time. "Lacey?" He was surprised by the depth of concern in his voice.

"I'm fine. Continue."

But she didn't sound fine, and her smile was forced. What had just happened? "Do you need a break?"

She shook her head, meeting his gaze, her expression unfathomable. "Not at all. Why? Do you need one?"

He recognised determination when he saw it. He smiled at her. "Not at all, but let me know if you can't manage and I'll let you sit down by a fire for a few minutes. I'll even fetch you a rug for your lap."

Lacey's eyes narrowed. "I'll show you who's old, grandpa." She renewed her attacks, flying around the room with increased energy.

Talon laughed, meeting every attack with all he had. This is what he wanted. This is what his wings had stolen from him. The energy that coursed through him screaming that he was alive. Alive and free. An hour wasn't going to be long enough.

Chapter Seventeen

Brianne paced her room, glancing once again at her locked door. What was she going to do? How had her family expected her to be able to find anything out? If she left the fortress she risked never being able to return. And every time she searched the fortress Talon seemed to be there, stopping her from finding anything important. He had an uncanny ability of turning up each time she found something that might be worth checking out.

A loud rap on her door brought her pacing to a halt. Her stomach flipped and her heart leapt. She'd been thinking all night about how to play out this scene and she still wasn't certain what to do. Now there was no more time for thinking. Hesitant steps brought her across the room and her hand hovered over the lock.

Another knock, then a voice spoke quietly and she strained to hear the words. "I'm so nervous that I couldn't have done this on my own. What if she isn't my daughter? How do I continue to wait and wonder? You have my eternal gratitude for coming with me, Holy Father."

Relief rushed through Brianne as she realised how she could play this scene. This was her opportunity to apply to read the archives. Surely she'd find something useful there. Before she had a chance to unlock the door, a familiar voice destroyed her plan.

"It was providence that I returned from communing with the Lord and Lady when I did."

No. It couldn't be. But how many times had she heard him preach about abominations, particularly in the last couple of years. His voice haunted her nightmares. Her gaze searched the room as she stepped away from the door, the next knock sounding louder and more impatient. She had to get out of here somehow. Her initial search had shown her what she already knew. There was only one exit and the Supreme One was at it, ready to accuse her of being an abomination. What was he doing here?

Her gaze stopped at the narrow window and she

quietly dashed across the room as her door shuddered. It looked like they were going to break it down. She looked out the window to the drop below. With wings she could have made it. Beyond the fortress was the city wall, the Feronian Mountains rising up in the distance. The door shuddered again. She had to do something. Anything was better than waiting to be caught. She looked down and this time noticed the narrow ledge that ran below her window and across the wall towards Talon's window.

She could make it. The journey looked easier than climbing to the top of her favourite rock pillar. Clambering over the sill, she pressed herself against the wall, her fingers searching out holds in between the stones. She inched along, keeping her gaze trained on Talon's window as it came closer. Her heart beat loudly and she fought the urge to turn and see if they'd breached her door and were looking out the window. Then she was climbing in Talon's window and landing on his floor to stare open mouthed at him prone on the floor, black wings spread out about him. This was impossible.

"Talon?"

His head rose and he stared at her, his face drawn by pain. "No." His word was a plea and his head sank again, his forehead pressed to the stone floor.

Thinking of the black feather she kept in her belt pouch, Brianne crossed the room. Kneeling before him her hands reached out to touch the side of his face and then his back where his wings emerged. Heat rose from his body, her hand feeling cold in comparison. "You're killing yourself." Her words were soft.

He raised his head to look at her. "I'm dead no matter how you look at it."

"I can help you if you'll help me." She continued to speak quietly, her hands kneading his back around his wings. "You're keeping them retracted too much. It's poisoning your body." There was a pounding at Talon's door, neither of them paid any attention.

"I can't spend the rest of my life hiding in my room so I can leave them out. How do you know it's poisoning me?" He continued to stay pressed against the floor, only his head raised. He groaned. "And how did you learn this? The pain's going already."

She drew her hands back and watched as he sat up, keeping her voice quiet. "Hide me. Tell them you haven't seen me and I'll help you."

"How do you know about wings?"

She didn't have time for this. Barrett was bellowing Talon's name through the door, warning him he'd break it down if he didn't let him in. "Please."

"Who are you, and don't tell me Lacey or you don't know. Don't give me any more lies."

"Brianne Devin."

"And who in the Infernal World is that?"

"A Caelian."

Talon drew back from her, swearing.

Brianne reached for him. "Please. At least give me a chance to explain myself. You can always hand me over to them later. Talon, please. I can help you."

He stared at her a moment longer before he roared, "What? I'm busy painting. Come back later." He rose to his feet, his wings retracting.

"Talon?" Brianne rose also.

"Set the canvas up." He pointed to the canvas leaning face first against the wall near an easel.

Barrett continued to bellow demands through the door, slamming something against it so it shuddered.

She put the canvas on the easel, wincing at the splash of colours randomly slashed across the painting. No wonder his father didn't believe he was an artist. Talon pushed her to the side, his shirt on and half buttoned, to splash some more random colours across the canvas.

He turned to her. "Get in the trunk at the foot of my bed."

She met his gaze, brown eyes seeming sincere,

but she didn't know for certain. What choice did she have? With a nod, she strode to the trunk that would either be her death or her salvation. Once she was pressed against the clothes in the bottom of the trunk, Talon threw a light blanket over her and closed the lid, plunging her into darkness. A shudder went through her as she heard it lock. Panic closely followed. She took deep breaths, closing her eyes as she tried to remain calm. It felt like she'd stepped willingly into a trap.

"What?" She heard Talon demand again.

"About time. What were you doing?"

"Isn't it obvious? Painting. How am I ever meant to get it finished with all these interruptions?"

Brianne wished she could see what was going on when the silence dragged out, then was glad she couldn't since that meant she was hidden.

"Sorry, Holy Father, I didn't realise you were there. My apologies. I would have opened the door immediately if I'd known."

"And yet you would not for your own father?" The Supreme One asked.

"The Lord and Lady say we should worship them with our talents and yet everyone continues to interrupt me."

Brianne couldn't help smiling at Talon's words.

She could imagine how annoyed the Supreme One was. He might be completely cloaked but he still managed to convey his feelings with his tone and the way he held his body.

"Enough of this insolence. Have you seen the girl?" Barrett demanded.

"Lacey?"

"Yes Lacey. Have you seen her?"

"Not since last night when we all dined together. She has a tendency to get lost in the fortress. Have you looked around for her?" Talon asked.

"Of course I've got people looking for her, but her door was locked from the inside."

"Did you check out the window? Maybe she got sick of not knowing who she is and jumped." There was a pause before Talon said, "I'm sorry Mistress, I didn't realise. I didn't mean to offend you."

Brianne wondered what the woman had said or done to cause the apologetic tone in Talon's voice. It was frustrating not knowing exactly what was happening out there.

"You will help find her," Barrett ordered.

"I'm in the middle of painting. Surely you have enough lackeys to run around after you. What about Bellamy?" Talon's words were met with silence.

Brianne remained cramped in the trunk,

wondering what was happening. She could hear nothing. Were they gone? What was he doing? Was he planning to leave her in here forever? Then she heard the click of the lock and the lid was thrown back, the blanket dragged from her.

She sat up to stare at Talon, his shirt still half buttoned. He remained silent, his gaze roaming over her as if he was trying to figure out all her secrets. A glance around the room showed they were alone, the door closed and hopefully locked. Her gaze returned to Talon who continued to watch her.

"You owe me some answers."

Rising to her feet, she stepped out of the trunk. "Let them out. Don't keep your wings retracted until you're half blind with pain."

"I can't risk keeping them out all the time."

"You can't risk not letting them out. I was serious when I said you're poisoning your body." She continued to watch him.

"It's only been the last few months that I've had control over them. I can keep them retracted more so I'm not spending most of my time in my room. I can't live the rest of my life shut up in here." He made a vague gesture to his room.

"You'd rather die?"

After a moment he unbuttoned his shirt, letting it

drop to the ground. His eyes closed and he threw his head back as his wings burst free. More minutes passed before his gaze met hers. "How do your people survive this pain?"

"There is no pain when you're not feather poisoned." She reached out to touch his wings, drawn by the dark feathers she longed to own.

He grabbed hold of her hand before she made contact. "You better be telling the truth."

"You don't know how lucky you are. I'd give anything to have wings."

Talon laughed, a harsh abrupt sound. "You're the one who's lucky. I'd give anything to be rid of them."

With the one hand still trapped, she reached out with the other, her fingertips connecting with his skin. Heat radiated from his shoulder. "You can't keep retracting them. They're killing you. Can't you feel the heat of the poison burning through you?"

"Didn't you say you were going to help me?" At her nod, Talon continued. "Then you can start with telling me what you're doing here."

Brianne lowered her hand, wishing now that she'd spent the time in the trunk planning what to tell him.

Chapter Eighteen

Talon sat on the edge of the trunk at the foot of his bed, head in his hands, his wings still out. He didn't know if he should believe a single word she'd said. He raised his head to meet her gaze. She sat cross-legged on his bed watching him. "The Supreme One? The Holy Father?"

Brianne nodded.

"You lie."

"I swear by the Lord and Lady your Supreme One is the same as ours."

"Impossible."

"I don't know what's going on, but something obviously is. And he's the only one who's trusted by both your father and my uncle. Actually, he's trusted by all our people. Yours and mine."

It couldn't be possible. He was the Supreme One, upholder of the Sacred Law, adviser to the War Leader and Political Leader. He knew everything about his people. Every single question he asked was answered without hesitation. "Prove it."

"I've been trying to prove it, well, prove something anyway. Someone has been passing information between our people, that's why I was sent here."

"That isn't proof. You want me to betray my people and let you live and do it all on trust. You're a liar. Obviously. And a good actress. How am I meant to believe a single word you say?"

She leaned towards him. "Then help me find the proof."

He looked away from her, shifting as he tried to find a comfortable way to sit with his wings out. "You could be saying that so you can find the information you were sent here for."

"You need a stool to sit on. That's what we use."

"And how would I explain that to anyone who asks?"

Brianne shrugged, then smiled. "You need it for your art. So you can sit at the easel while you create your masterpiece."

He glared at her, anger rushing through him at the reminder of his failure.

"I'm sorry. If only we'd been born to the opposite people. Can you use a bow?"

"I use a crossbow. What has that to do with anything?"

"I was just wondering if you'd have outperformed Macklyn in every skill like I did." She fell silent a moment before she added softly, "Until he grew wings."

"Of course I would've done better than your Macklyn." His glare remained in place. "Especially if he couldn't beat you."

Brianne started to laugh, then smothered it with her hand, glancing towards the door. "How does that ego manage to fit in bed beside you each night?"

"You can change the topic as much as you like, but it won't change that I don't trust you."

Brianne's smile faded. "I don't think you trust anyone." Her gaze was drawn to his wings. "You don't really have a choice. You need what I know or you won't live much longer. Haven't you noticed it's getting harder to keep them retracted? That the pain is worse and the days seem to be getting hotter. You're suffering from feather poisoning. Some of my people get it when they're first learning to control their wings and misjudge how long they can keep them retracted." Her gaze held his. "You help me and

I'll help you. I promise I won't take any information back to my people that you don't want them to have."

"I don't want them to have any information."

"And what about the Supreme One? If he's playing us against each other, don't you want them to know? What if every battle fought has been due to his interference?"

"Every battle fought has been because you've been trying to steal our land."

Brianne shook her head. "No, every battle fought has been because your people came over the mountains and drove us out of our lands."

"Your people came from the sea and tried to take our lands from us."

"Have you seen the ocean around our part of the land? That's impossible. The shoreline is filled with rock spires and the winds swirl and slam us against them. The only way out to sea is near the Feronian Mountains and you have those areas heavily guarded. We've even tried reaching the mountains, but you always prevent us. You want us forced to keep trying to make barren land grow crops while your fields nearly overflow with food."

Talon slowly shook his head, trying to make sense of it all. He'd been raised on tales of the invasion. Been told a million times that to let the Caelians reach the Feronian Mountains was to be surrounded by the enemy. Lacey, no, Brianne seemed so sincere. But she always had. He reached out and lifted her hand, comparing the pale brown to his own golden brown tones.

"Vieteh berries."

He let her hand drop. "Is it any wonder I can't trust you? Even your skin lies."

"So does my hair and eyes. But my words are true. Please let me prove them to you."

"How?"

"I don't know."

He stared at her for long moments before he rose to his feet to pace the room. "I can't keep you here. If I'm caught hiding you they'll kill me along with you."

"You better hope they don't find me because I know your secret."

His heart sank. His life might be miserable and barely worth living, but he wasn't about to give it up. He only had one choice. He drew his sword.

"I won't go quiet. You might want to rethink this."

"You have no sword." He advanced.

Brianne grinned fleetingly. "You think that'll matter?" She backed away. "You're a warrior too, you tell me what you'd do in the same situation. What would you do to protect your people?"

"Anything."

"Me too. Except Macklyn. I'll let you have him. The rest I'll protect with my life." She reached the table and four chairs near the wall, grabbing a chair to hold in front of her.

"You seem pretty obsessed with this Macklyn considering you want him dead."

"Probably about as obsessed as you are with Bellamy." Another fleeting grin. "Did you think I didn't notice?" She stepped to the side and away from the wall. "Come on Talon. Put down your weapon and let's figure this out."

"You know you can't beat me."

"Actually, I can. I know your weaknesses now and you don't have a clue. You won't know how to defend them." Her gaze rose to his wings then back to his face. "Give me a couple of days. Work with me on this. We have to find out why the Supreme One is doing this. There has to be a reason."

"What weaknesses?"

"You've got to be kidding. Do you really think I'm going to tell you?"

"Tell me one of them and I'll think about helping you."

"Sure you will. Why should I trust you any more than you want to trust me?"

He lowered his sword, not knowing what to do. He swore. Once again his wings were ruining his life. "You shouldn't." He concentrated on trying to retract his wings.

"No. Don't. Talon, you're killing yourself." She came towards him, putting the chair down as she did. "Talon." She pressed her palms against his cheeks.

He closed his eyes, her hands cold against the heat of his skin. "I was dead the moment I became an infernal bird." He opened his eyes to meet her gaze when she slid her hands down to his chest, sliding them around to his back and the ridges there. Her hands pressed against the ridges and he fought to keep his wings retracted. "What are you trying to do?" His sword fell to the ground as pain rushed through him.

"Save you." Her arms tightened when he tried to pull away.

Then his wings were free and he stumbled back as she let him go. They refused to retract. "What did you do?"

"It'll be at least half an hour before they retract." She bent and picked up his sword, holding it at her side.

His gaze scanned the room checking for weapon

options while most of his attention stayed on Brianne. He should have killed her while he had the chance, but he hadn't been able to bring himself to do it. His father never would have shown such weakness towards the enemy.

Stepping back, Brianne laid the sword across her palms, keeping them close to her body. She stared at him a moment more before she held it out as she spoke. "Promise to help me save our people."

His gaze was drawn from the sword to her eyes that continued to watch him steadily. A million thoughts went through his mind, but it was her words that echoed in his head the loudest. Save our people. He stepped forward and rested his palms against the sword, directly above hers. "Yes."

Chapter Nineteen

Brianne

Brianne felt like hitting Talon. "Can't you stay still?"

"You're the one who told me I have to sleep with my wings out the entire night. I sleep on my side, not my stomach. I feel like the bed's suffocating me."

"I'll be suffocating you if you don't let me get some sleep." She tugged at the rope that was attached to both her wrist and the bed head, lying fully clothed beside Talon. Even her boots were still on. "I don't see why you had to tie me up. I said I wouldn't run." She had no idea how she was meant to convince him that he could trust her. At least on the issue of her sticking around until they found out what was going on.

"Shut up. It's hard enough to try and sleep without you talking all night."

"It's nearly morning," Brianne muttered.

"Then shut up and let me sleep. I had enough problems to deal with before you came along and added to them."

"Wings aren't a problem. I'd give anything to be able to fly."

There was a long moment of silence before Talon answered. "I can't fly."

Brianne sat up to look at his shadowy figure in the dark, wishing it was brighter so she could see his expression. "What do you mean you can't fly?"

"Exactly that."

"You mean you're not very good at it."

Talon sat up as well. "No, I can't fly." He growled, "How in the Infernal World am I meant to sit up with these things out?"

"Sit on the edge of the bed." She frowned. "You've never flown. Ever."

"Haven't even flapped my wings."

She ignored the thread of bitterness in his tone. "Are you deliberately trying to kill yourself, or is it a natural skill you have?"

"What's wrong now?"

"They're like any other muscle. You need to exercise them. I'm surprised you aren't already dead."

"You and me both," he muttered.

"You have to exercise them."

"How?"

"The mountains aren't far from here. You could practice flying there."

"They're nearly an hour away."

"That's not far." When he didn't answer, she continued. "I'm serious Talon. You have to exercise them."

"You want me to get caught."

"No, I don't. I need your help to save our people." She almost felt guilty for having used that line to convince him yesterday, except it was true. Or at least she guessed it was. Surely her grandfather and uncle wouldn't have sent her in without telling her the Supreme One was also a spy for them. She remembered Barrett's comment about her people having removed identity tags for the past couple of months. Pushing that uncomfortable thought from her mind she said, "Talon? You still listening?" He continued to sit across from her, a shadow in the darkened room.

"Go to sleep." He rose from the bed and crossed the room to stand by the window.

Brianne carefully slid the dagger from her boot. With another look in Talon's direction to make sure he continued to stare out the window, she cut the rope, sheathed the dagger and followed him. "What's wrong? Are you in pain?" She pressed a hand against his back, between his wings, feeling the unnatural heat of his skin.

"I'm always in pain, it's only the degree that varies." He reached out to her hand, sliding his across her wrist and the rope still tied there, the end dangling. "Give me your dagger."

She tugged her hand free. "What dagger?"

"I'm not in the mood for this."

"I used my teeth to gnaw through the rope."

"Brianne." There was a warning in his tone.

"Talon." She mimicked his tone, refusing cower. He reached for her again and she stepped away. "I can show you some flying exercises."

"After you give me the dagger."

"Would you hand over your dagger?"

The silence stretched out and then he sighed. "Show me the exercises."

She stared at him suspiciously. "And the dagger?"

"You can keep it for now. What's a dagger compared to a sword?"

Brianne grinned, glad of the darkness. He had no idea and she planned to keep it that way. "Come to the middle of the room, you're going to need plenty of space for these exercises." She watched as he lit a candle before joining her.

When the first rays of morning light struggled into the room, they were still going. Brianne stared at the pain and fatigue that etched Talon's face. "How about we try and get some sleep now?"

"No. Not until I get these right."

No wonder she'd known what to say to convince him yesterday. They were far too alike. "Well maybe if you weren't such a slow learner we'd be done by now."

"Show me," he growled.

When he did the exercise more accurately, she was barely able to hold back her grin. Yes, they were very much alike. Another couple of attempts and it was close to perfect. "Now can we get some sleep?" She waited for him to answer. When the silence dragged out and he continued to stare at her, she asked, "Well?"

"If I get hold of some penitent robes for you, do you think you can get into the House of the Lord and Lady and find proof?"

She didn't hesitate. "Yes."

"Are you certain?"

She'd make sure she was. "Of course I am."

"I'll get robes for you during the day and when

it's dark I'll lower you out the window. Guards never bother patrolling the back of the fortress because there's no way into it unless you have help from inside." He stared at her a moment longer. "You better return."

"Unless I'm caught I'll return."

"Don't you dare get caught."

Brianne looked away from his gaze. That wasn't something she could promise. Her gaze fell on the bed. "Sleep now?" She turned back to him and when he nodded, crossed the room to drop onto the bed, keeping her boots on in case she needed to make a quick exit. She watched as he walked towards her, his wings cloaking him. How she ached to have wings. It wasn't right that a Tersten should have them when she didn't.

Once he blew out the candle, Talon stopped at the edge of the bed. "What?"

"They're so beautiful."

"They'll be my death." He lowered himself onto the bed, lying on his stomach with his head turned towards her.

She reached out and ran a finger across several feathers. "They'd be worth it." With her hand resting against his wing, she closed her eyes and drifted off to sleep.

Chapter Twenty

Talon

Talon waited until his father left his office before he entered, having pottered around in the corridor with one of his paintings, pretending to find the perfect place to hang it. The only attention his father gave him when he strode past was a look of disgust mingled with disappointment.

Seeing the office was empty he opened the door to the right of the entrance and stepped into the small room, lit only by a barred window, closing the door of the storage room behind him. An old desk, trunks, and several stacks of paper and books filled the barely used room. Talon headed straight for the desk, sliding open the bottom drawer, relieved to find the old key still there. He dropped it into his belt pouch, smiling slightly as he recalled the prank he and Marshall had planned for the laundry years ago. It hadn't turned out exactly as they'd expected. They'd made a copy of the key and when they'd tried to sneak into the laundry late one night, about six years ago, someone had been in there. Running back to the fortress, they'd hidden the key in the storage room, planning to try again another night. It had never happened. Each of them had made excuses until the key was forgotten when more interesting things came along.

About to leave the room, still holding his painting, Talon froze as he heard a sound in the office. He pressed his ear against the door. It was quiet. Should he open the door and check? He reached for the handle.

"Are you sure this is what she looks like?"

Talon pulled his hand away from the door at the sound of the Supreme One's voice.

"The soldier I had draw her likeness is a talented artist and he's seen her a few times, Elden."

Talon frowned. Who else was with his father and the Supreme One? He'd never heard an Elden mentioned before.

"You have to find her. You can't let her escape. She's the niece of their First Officer," the Supreme One said.

"She was examined. They found no wings," Barrett said.

"She's an abomination," the Supreme One said.

Barrett swore and Talon wondered when Elden would speak, but it was his father who spoke next. "Why didn't you warn me there was an abomination, Elden?"

"I didn't think she'd be a problem," the Supreme One snapped.

Talon stared at the door, wishing he could see who was with his father. Who was Elden and why hadn't he answered the question directed at him? He didn't like the suspicion that was starting to form.

"You said you'd help us in our fight against them. Why aren't we winning?" Barrett demanded.

"You can't let her escape," the Supreme One said.

"Stop ordering me around, Elden. I'm not your lackey."

His father's words filled him with dread. Placing the painting against a nearby trunk, he lay on the floor to peer under the door.

"Without me, all your people would be dead. I'm keeping you alive," the Supreme One said. "Don't you dare forget it. The Prilonians would wipe you out if you were no longer of use to them."

He could only see his father's boots and the edge of the black robe of the Supreme One.

"I've kept my part of the bargain, you better keep yours."

There was a short silence before the Supreme One answered Barrett. "Don't let the girl escape." He strode to the door, the hem of his robes swirling around him.

Talon continued to lie on the floor, peering under the door. He watched as his father remained in place for several minutes before he swore and left the office, closing his door behind him. Talon searched as much of the office as he could see, the desk obstructing very little of his view of the floor. He was almost certain there was no one else in the room. Rising slowly to his feet, he cautiously opened the door, looking around. It was empty.

Rubbing at the ridges on his shoulder blades, he tried to ease the tightness and pain that was starting to build. What was his father thinking? And who were the Prilonians? Should he be helping Brianne? It sounded like the Supreme One was on their side. But if he was, why weren't they winning?

Grabbing his painting, Talon closed the storage room door before he eased the door to the corridor open. Seeing it empty, he hurried out, almost running back to his room, mentally arguing with himself over what he should do. He didn't know if he should still get robes for Brianne, but he didn't have to decide immediately. The laundry staff wouldn't start making deliveries and collecting the next day's dirty linen from the House, hospital and fortress until after lunch.

Reaching his door, he checked the corridor before he knocked, using the prearranged code, and waited for Brianne to let him in. As soon as she opened it, he slid inside, locking the door behind him. Staring at her, he tried to decide what to do.

"Couldn't you get any robes?"

"I've got a key to the laundry, but I can't go until this afternoon."

"Then what went wrong?"

Talon placed his painting face first against the wall near the door, not taking his gaze from Brianne. "How do you know something went wrong?"

"Because you look like you lost a war, not won a battle."

He stared at her a moment longer before he looked away and crossed the room to drop onto the edge of his bed. His back tightened and he fought against letting his wings free. They'd only get in his way.

"Talon?" Brianne came to stand in front of him.

When he looked up at her, she asked, "What happened?"

"Do you know the Supreme One's name?"

She shook her head. "They have to give up their names, their families and their identities to join the House."

"Have you heard the name Elden before?" When she shook her head again, he asked, "What about Prilonians?"

Again she shook her head. "What happened?"

He rose to his feet and started to cross the room to the window. He stopped and looked back at her. "I have no idea."

"What do you think happened?"

"Either my father is a traitor or the Supreme One is working against your people." He carefully watched her expression. It didn't change.

"If the Supreme One's working for your people then why aren't you winning? He has access to everything my people know and plan except for me being here."

That was exactly what he wanted to know. What in the name of the Master of the Infernal World was his father up to? Whatever it was, it didn't seem to be helping their people to win.

Chapter Twenty-One

Brianne

Brianne paced the room, alone for the second time that day. Frustration filled her at the small pieces of information Talon had given her. How was she meant to figure this out if he didn't share what he discovered? And how was she meant to learn anything locked in Talon's room all the time?

Her pacing was brought to a stop by a knock at the door. It wasn't Talon. She didn't even know how long it would be before he returned. Surely he couldn't be too much longer. Another knock. She stared at the door, wishing she had a better weapon than the dagger in her boot.

"Talon," Garnet called through the door. "Let me in, Talon." She knocked again, then tried the doorknob.

Brianne nearly groaned. She had no way of getting rid of her.

Another knock. "Come on, Talon. Let me in. I need to talk to you." Silence. "Talon." Impatience filled her tone as she pounded on the door. "Talon." This time her voice was filled with surprise. "Who's in your room?"

"What do you want, Garnet?"

At Talon's voice, Brianne quietly stepped up to the door to press her ear against it.

"I can't find Lacey and our father won't tell me anything. Do you know where she is?"

"Don't try and find her, Garnet. Everyone's looking for her. You don't want to be mixed up in this."

"You know what's going on, don't you?"

"No. The little I know makes me wonder at how much I don't know. Promise me you'll stay out of this."

"Why?"

"Promise me, Garnet."

Brianne could hear the urgency in his voice and wondered what it was like to have a sibling.

"She's my friend."

"She's a Caelian."

There was a moment of silence before Garnet

answered. "I don't believe you. She doesn't have wings."

"Trust me on this. She's a Caelian."

"They'll kill her when they find her, won't they?"

When there was only silence, Brianne wished she could see what was happening.

"Talon? Will they?"

He finally answered. "Yes."

"You've got to find her. Don't let them get her."

"She's a Caelian."

"So? She's my friend."

Brianne's eyes closed as she drew in a shaky breath, trying to remind herself they were the enemy. The thought seemed false and her heart wasn't in it.

"What if everything she told you was a lie? Everything she did was a lie. She's a spy for our enemy, Garnet."

"I don't believe that. When you find her, ask her."

"Garnet–"

"Don't let them kill her. You want me to stay out of it, then promise me that."

Brianne held her breath waiting for his answer. It seemed to take an age to arrive.

"I promise." Silence met his words. Eventually the silence was broken by Talon speaking quietly. "Open the door, Brianne."

She unlocked the door and let him in. She watched him as he locked the door, dropped a sack on the floor and started to unbutton his shirt. He didn't speak and she didn't know what to ask him. Once his wings were free, she found the words she needed to say. "Not everything was a lie."

Talon continued to meet her gaze, not speaking. She wondered if he was in too much pain to answer and started to reach out for him to check his temperature. He stepped to the side and strode to the middle of the room, his back to her, and began the exercises she'd taught him.

Since he didn't say, she decided to find out for herself. Reaching for the sack, she opened it and stared at the reddish-brown robes. Closing the sack she dropped it to the floor, fear and excitement rushing through her. She had to find something. It didn't matter what. Something that explained exactly what was going on. She strode to the bed and watched Talon as he continued his flying exercises. How she wished she was doing them with him, her wings outstretched as she worked on strengthening them and gaining control over them in preparation for her first flight. She dropped backwards onto the bed to stare at the ceiling. It wasn't fair. Everyone got wings but her. Her view was blocked by Talon towering over her.

"What's wrong? Are you worried about tonight? If you don't think you're up to it, we'll come up with another plan."

She shook her head, feeling slightly offended that he thought she might not be up to the task. "No. I can't wait." She hesitated, she'd told him more than enough lies. Sitting up, she took a deep breath before she offered him the truth. "I wish I had your wings. I've trained my entire life to join a squad and eventually lead it."

"I'd get rid of mine if I could. I've trained my entire life to lead a unit and become general after my father retires." He held out his hand to her. "Train with me. We'll use daggers. It should be quieter."

Placing her hand in his, she let him pull her to her feet, a smile forming. "I wouldn't count on it, but maybe we should work on teaching you how to use your wings in battle. If we have an enemy out there we're going to need every advantage."

Talon let go of her hand and pulled a dagger from his boot. "If we have an enemy out there I can't understand why my father would surrender to them and not fight to the last person."

Brianne drew out her own dagger. "None of my

people would let an enemy dictate what we can do. No matter what the odds. Even the fledglings would fight for our freedom."

Chapter Twenty-Two

Talon

Talon slipped inside his room, dropping a sack next to the one he'd brought back earlier that day. He turned to face Brianne, searching her face for any signs of fear. "Are you ready?" He gestured towards the sack. "We've got rope."

Brianne slowly smiled, excitement lighting her eyes. "I've been ready all day. You're the one who's taken forever to gather the gear we need."

He recognised the look in her eyes, it echoed the way he felt. "Then let's go. Put on your robe." He threw the other sack to her.

"You're coming too?"

"I'll be nearby."

"How are you going to get down?"

"Fly."

Brianne shook her head. "You can't. Asking a thousand questions isn't the same as knowing how to fly."

"I guess I'll find out soon enough." He started to remove his shirt and bandages.

"Are you crazy?"

"One of those vests you told me your people wear would be good right now." He tied his shirt at his waist before he took the rope from the sack.

"Talon." Brianne reached out to him.

He stepped past her, avoiding her hand. "Unless you've changed your mind, let's do this." He shrugged off her hand when it finally landed on his shoulder.

"I know what to do to keep your wings retracted."

He spun to face her. "Don't even think about it."

"You'll kill yourself."

"I thought you said I was killing myself anyway." How hard could it be to fly? If the Caelians could do it, there was no reason he couldn't.

"Don't worry about flying. Once you step out that window, spread your wings as far as you can, then beat them very slowly. You'll kind of glide to the ground." She eyed him up and down. "Or at least you should, but you have a more solid build than my people. At least you're not as solid looking as most

Terstens. If you were that heavy you'd probably drop like a rock."

She said it like it was a bad thing. Who wanted to look like they could be easily snapped in two? "Put the robe and gloves on so we can get moving." He strode towards the window and tied the rope to the thick stick he'd collected earlier, bracing it against the wall on either side of the window before he threw the rope outside.

Brianne stopped beside him, resting her gloved hand on his arm, the hood of her robe pushed back. "You don't have to come. Take your first flight another day. Preferably from the ground."

"Are you still going to do this or should I do it myself?"

"You're too tall to pass for a penitent." She frowned. "I never realised that before. None of them are much taller than me and I know people who've joined the House of the Lord and Lady that are a lot taller than I am."

So did he, but they had other things they needed to focus on. "You're wasting darkness." He held the stick steady while she clambered onto the window ledge.

She stared at him for a moment, perched on the window ledge, her hands clinging to the frame.

"Don't kill yourself." She lowered herself over the edge, making her way down the rope.

Talon waited until she was partway down before he climbed onto the ledge, facing his room. Holding onto the window frame, he leaned backwards out the window. It took several painful moments before his wings burst forth and he let go, stretching his wings out as far as he could. The ground rushed up to him. He felt a moment of fear and pumped his wings hard. Then the ground was rapidly receding so he slowed the movements. He cursed when he slowed his wings too much and again the ground came rushing at him. A little more wing speed had him finally landing on the ground, staggering as he came to a stop.

Brianne threw herself at him, her arms sliding around him, a palm resting high on his back between his wings. "I thought you were going to die. I can't believe you did that."

Over the initial fear, he grinned. "Actually, it wasn't too bad. I think I'll have to try that again."

"Now?" She drew away from him.

He laughed at her expression of disbelief, clear enough even in the shadows. "Later. After we see what you can find in the House."

Once Talon had retracted his wings and put his shirt on they travelled quietly through the streets, avoiding several units that were searching for Brianne. The area around the House of the Lord and Lady was quiet, dark and deserted.

He reached out to take her hand and pull her back to him when she started for the entrance. "Be careful in there. Don't take any chances and get out if you think it's too dangerous."

"Like you with your flying?"

Talon laughed softly. "I'm still alive. I bet your Macklyn couldn't have done so well."

"He's not mine. I gave him to you. Remember?"

"Are you trying to put off going inside? Have you changed your mind?"

"A million times, but I'll still go through with it. I need to find out how much danger our people are in."

"Good luck." He held out his hand to her.

She looked from his hand to his face several times before she spoke. "My people don't offer to shake hands in situations like this." She leaned forward and kissed first one cheek and then the other. "That's how friends wish each other luck in Caelis. As well as say hello and goodbye." She pulled her hood up, hiding her grin as she turned away from him.

He stared after her as she ran across the space between him and the entrance. She better be careful in there. It wasn't like he had a disguise he could use to rescue her if she got into trouble.

Looking around he spotted a place in the shadows where he could wait and still see the entrance. He'd barely hidden when a unit marched past, lanterns swinging as they continued their search for Brianne. His father was going to be in a foul mood when they failed to find her.

Chapter Twenty-Three

Brianne

Brianne slipped through the door behind the altar, thinking there were far too many candles burning. A little darkness wouldn't hurt. A glance showed no one was in the room. More candles burned in ornate holders and a table was set off to one side, a trunk nearby. It was the stairs leading to the rooms below the House that drew her attention. Worn stone stairs wide enough for several people to walk abreast.

She approached them cautiously, trying to remind herself that she had the perfect disguise, but it wasn't really. If someone talked to her she had no idea what to say, or how to act. A look down the stairs showed they were empty. Hurrying down them, she checked every corner of the small room they led to. The room was an empty stairwell, several doors leading out from it. All of them closed. Taking a deep breath, she strode to the nearest door, determined to find something.

A corridor led away from the stairwell, lit by lanterns hung from the ceiling. She paused at each door along the corridor, listening at them. A few had soft voices behind them, some were silent. She had no idea what was behind each door or if she should open them. When she reached the end of the corridor, she faced the final room. There was silence behind the closed door. Testing the doorknob, she found it unlocked. Slowly easing it open, she closed it again when she saw a sleeping figure in an ornate bed.

Her heart beat fast and adrenaline rushed through her as she quietly spun and hurried along the corridor, hoping she hadn't disturbed the sleeping person. Back in the stairwell, she chose a different door. Finding another empty corridor she sped along it, wondering how much time she'd wasted. Was Talon safe? Had anyone found him? Would it matter if they did? Surely he could offer some plausible reason for wandering around out there at this hour of the night.

She reached the end of the corridor and tried the doorknob, turning it and peeking through the gap. It seemed to be an office. She swung the door open further and seeing it empty stepped inside. Leaving the door open since the room wasn't lit, she looked around. A desk sat to one side, a carved and cushioned chair behind it, two wooden chairs in front. Shelves ran along one wall filled with leather bound books and on the far wall, between two trunks, was a door.

Brianne stepped back into the corridor and lifted the closest lantern down from a hook before she returned to the office and shut the door. A check showed that there was no lock on the door. She eyed the two ornate candleholders sitting on each side of the door on small, carved tables, but decided to leave their candles unlit. The lantern cast enough light.

Placing the lantern on the middle of the desk, she opened drawers, rummaging through them. There were letters addressed to Elden, the Holy Father and the Supreme One. Dread filled her. A sound brought her to her feet and around to the other side of the desk as the door swung in towards her.

A brown robed Elder stepped into the room. "What are you doing in here?"

Playing a hunch, Brianne slowly moved towards him as she said, "Elden told me to bring something to him. That he'd meet me here in a few minutes."

"Elden is asleep. Has been for at least an hour."

Brianne shook her head, glad for the robes that completely hid her. "He isn't now. Oh look, here he comes." She pointed behind him, reaching for one of the candleholders as he turned to look. Taking a deep breath she swung the candleholder, bringing it down hard on his head. He crumpled at her feet and she dragged him into the office, closing the door behind them. Staring at the door, she listened for any sounds. It was quiet. She was still safe.

Bending down, she tugged away the hood of the Elder's robe and stared at him. Curly brown hair, freckled skin and when she lifted an eyelid, green eyes. This man wasn't a Caelian or a Tersten. She stripped his robe from him and tearing it, used it to bind his hands and feet and gag him. He wore trousers and a linen shirt that was embroidered in an unfamiliar pattern. His belt pouch contained several coins and a linen handkerchief. Some of the coins were familiar, ones she'd grown up using. Bunching up her robe she put the coins in her belt pouch so she could show them to Talon. Caelian coins shouldn't be in Terst. There wasn't a single reason for them to be here. The only personal items that squads took into battle were their weapons. They didn't take anything else and that included money.

Hands on her hips, she stared down at the man. She had to do something with him. If someone else came through that door they'd see him instantly. Grabbing him under the arms, she dragged him behind the desk, where he'd be hidden if someone else opened the door. At least until they came around the desk. She turned her attention back to the room. She couldn't leave Talon outside all night.

She leafed through several books, some of which were in a foreign language, then turned towards the trunks. They contained robes, parchments, strangely made clothes and weapons. She ran her fingers over the blunt ends of some throwing darts, unable to resist taking them and adding their leather case to her belt.

That left only the second door to search behind, but when she tried to turn the handle, she found it was locked. Grabbing a dagger from one of the trunks, she pried at the door. A broken lock would be no more obvious than a man tied and gagged in the corner. She levered the timber surrounds and the moment she thought the dagger might snap, the surrounds gave way, prying loose from the stone wall, the door swinging open.

Dropping the damaged dagger, Brianne grabbed the lantern and held it up at the doorway. Her gaze was drawn up and down the rows of crammed bookcases. How was she meant to find anything in here? And how much time did she have? She needed to be out before daylight.

Checking some of the nearest books, she returned them to the shelves. Randomly pulling books from shelves, she discarded them when they were either in a foreign language or about an uninteresting subject. The further she moved into the room, the older the books became. Staring at the gilded leather book in her hands, Brianne ran a finger over the cover before she looked to the far end. Still holding the book, she strode forward, hoping she'd find the oldest ones there.

She hesitantly reached for a book, relieved to find she was right, flicking through the pages before she grabbed another one. Some of the books contained faded pages, others pages that were torn or damaged. Picking up a couple of likely books, she started to walk away when she saw a thin, small book sitting on top of the books on the bottom shelf. Reaching for it, she noticed the pages were more worn then the rest, the handwriting full of loops and swirls and at the top of the first page was a date. The book was centuries old.

Grinning, she added the book to her small pile and headed back to the first room. She grabbed one of the strangely embroidered linen shirts from the trunk and wrapped the books in it, embroidery facing the inside of her parcel. About to leave the room, she returned, grabbed one of the books written in the foreign language in case it was one Talon recognised and a handful of letters from the desk, adding them to the bundle before stepping into the corridor.

It was still empty and she raced along the corridor, excitement rushing through her at a successful raid. A voice rang out behind her as she was about to enter the stairwell.

"Stop!"

A glance showed it was another brown robed Elder. She ignored the woman's order and ran for the stairs. The sound of feet pounded behind her as she ran past the altar and through the House. Outside a unit marched by, turning to face her as she ran into the street.

"Stop that penitent."

Brianne didn't need to look behind her to know it was the Elder. Changing directions, she raced towards the shadows, cries ringing out behind her. She had no idea where she was going, but she wasn't about to stop and ask for directions. Then a hand reached out and dragged her into a narrow street. She struggled, about to strike out with her free hand.

"Brianne."

She momentarily sagged against Talon, relief

rushing through her. "I've got books and letters. We have to get out of here."

"This way."

Pushing her hood back out of the way, she took hold of his hand, letting him lead the way, the sounds of pursuit close on their heels. Hopefully he knew a way out because she didn't have a clue where they were.

Chapter Twenty-Four

Talon

Talon ran, pain tearing through his back as his wings wanted to burst free. Gripping Brianne's hand tightly, he undid the buttons of his shirt, tearing it free to hang from the arm that dragged Brianne.

"Where are we going?"

"Over the wall."

"Are you kidding?" Brianne demanded. "You can't fly."

"I did earlier."

Brianne tugged on his arm. "Let me go. You take the books and I'll lead them away."

Talon tightened his grip. "No. Now shut up and run. We're nearly at the wall."

"We'll never make it over the top. You're not strong enough."

He opened his mouth to argue as they reached the walls. There was no time for arguments. They had to get out of here. "How do we do this?" When she didn't answer, he demanded, "Do you want to be caught?"

"You better not kill me," Brianne muttered before she turned her back to him, leaning against him. "Put your arms under mine, cross them over my chest and hold onto my shoulders."

He did as she said, pulling her against him as the sounds of men calling out and searching grew closer. "Now what?"

"Fly. Just don't kill me."

He wanted to ask how, but didn't think that would improve her confidence in his ability to fly. He did like he had before, moving his wings as fast as possible. They rose into the air, his shirt still dangling from one arm as they shot up beside the wall.

"Slower. You won't be able to keep up this pace," Brianne said.

The wall fell below them and he reduced his speed, still rising.

"Tilt your wings. What are you trying to do? Touch the moon?"

"I'm trying," he growled. His wings wouldn't

cooperate and they were beginning to ache. He faltered and instead of rising they began to fall.

"You'll kill us if we fall. Tilt your wings, Talon."

He heard the fear in her voice, but could do nothing about it. As hard as he tried, his wings wouldn't tilt. They continued to drop through the air, the wall coming closer.

"I told you that you wouldn't be able to fly. No wonder you quit the army. You probably couldn't last a full battle."

Anger stirred in him. If it wasn't for these infernal wings he'd still be in the army, she knew nothing. He beat harder and finally managed to tilt them slightly. They were above the wall.

"Drop slowly. Put us on the wall," Brianne ordered.

"I can get us over it," he said through clenched teeth.

"I didn't mean it. Just put us on the wall."

"Mean what." His wings ached, fatigue pulled at him and he was starting to drop again. Brianne squirmed in his arms and he swore as he struggled to hold her and keep flying. "Stay still."

"Put us down. Please, Talon. I know you could get us over the wall, but we need to be on it. Put us down."

He had no idea why they needed to be on the wall,

but at least she was willing to admit he could get them over it. He slowed, trying to put them down gently. The descent was a jerky, drop and rise motion.

They were nearly on the wall when Brianne said, "Let me go. Now."

She twisted in his arms and he had no choice but to let her fall the last few feet. She rolled, coming up on her feet, her bundle still clutched to her chest. His landing wasn't as graceful and he crashed into the hard stone on the top of the wall, cursing as he struggled to his feet, his wings in the way.

He retracted his wings to make it easier to rise to his feet. Facing Brianne, he tried to read her expression in the shadows, a hint of grey in the sky warning that day was on the way. "Why do we need to be up here?"

Brianne grinned. "Because you might be able to get us over the wall, but you wouldn't be able to get us back in again."

He glared at her, his earlier concern for her replaced with annoyance. "Very funny." Removing his shirt from his arm, he tied it around his waist. "What did you find? And what took you so long? It'll be daylight soon and we're stuck on top of the wall where we'll be caught by a patrol."

"I had to knock out one of the Elders and tie him up."

"You did what? You better enjoy your life while you can because when you die you're going to end up in the Infernal World."

Brianne shook her head, hiking up the skirt of her robe to reach into her belt pouch. "He wasn't one of us." She held out a handful of coins to him, letting her robe fall back into place. "These ones are Caelian. They were in his belt pouch." She pointed to some of the coins.

"How do you know he wasn't one of us?" Talon took the coins, leaving behind the ones she said were Caelian. He tilted his hand, trying to catch enough light to see what they were. Five of the coins he'd never seen before. "Are you sure these aren't Caelian?"

"Absolutely. And he wasn't like us. He had freckled skin, brown curly hair and green eyes."

Talon stared at her. "Are you sure? Maybe his eyes were murky brown, some of us have murky brown eyes and dark brown hair."

"His hair was light brown and his eyes were as green as summer grass. Do any of your people have freckled skin? Some of my people do, but not like him. Not a thousand of them scattered across his face and hands."

"Maybe he came from both of our people. Did you check for wings?" Talon put the coins in his belt pouch.

"No. But-" she broke off, swearing as she stepped past him, pulling her dagger from her boot.

Talon spun, drawing his sword from his scabbard as he did, his gaze running along the top of the wall with its raised edges blocking most of the view of what was below. Seeing nothing he looked skywards to spot a Caelian flying towards them, white wings stark against the grey light of the early morning. He stopped not far from them, remaining in the air above the wall.

"What are you doing here?" Brianne snarled.

"Who is he?" Talon demanded.

"Macklyn," Brianne said at the same time as the Caelian said, "None of your business, dirt walker."

"This is the one you said I could kill?" Talon asked.

"I didn't exactly say that. Just that I wouldn't protect him," Brianne said.

"I knew we shouldn't have trusted you." Macklyn drew his bow, aiming an arrow at them.

Brianne stepped in front of Talon, her dagger held

by the tip of the curved blade. "I've always been quicker than you, Macklyn."

Talon stepped to the side of her. "I don't need you to be my shield."

"It's not the type of dagger you're used to," Macklyn said.

"I've practised with it. Want to see how good I am?"

Talon heard a shout from below. "We've been spotted thanks to bird-boy."

"Wait until First Officer Ewyn hears of this." Macklyn started to rise higher into the air.

Brianne kept her dagger up. "Tell them the Supreme One is passing along information to General Barrett Morin, the Tersten leader."

"War Leader," Talon corrected.

"Lies. The Supreme One told me to guard against your words when he found out we were forced to spend time together." Macklyn continued to keep the arrow trained on them.

"What have you told him, Macklyn? If this mission fails it'll be your fault."

"We have to get off the wall." Talon forced his wings to snap out as he heard more shouts from below.

"If this mission fails it'll be no one's fault but yours."

Macklyn turned his gaze away from Brianne and pointed his finger at Talon. "And having wings doesn't make you less of a dirt walker." He turned and started to fly away.

Brianne screamed after him, "Tell them, Macklyn. Make sure you tell them."

Talon swore, turning to see men running towards him, the sky light enough to recognise the soldiers. He was dead. They were both dead.

Brianne slid her knife back into her boot, dragging the robe from herself, still holding the bundle. "You have to fly us out of here."

He watched as the distance between them and the soldiers shrank, his heart sinking as he saw one of them was Marshall. There was no way he could fight his own people. He sheathed his sword and waited for them to reach him, his wings stretched out, claiming the truth he'd tried to hide for so long.

Brianne grabbed his arm, shaking him. "Don't you dare give up."

He met angry brown eyes, seeing patches of murky blue-green in them. "I'm sorry. I can't fight my people."

"I won't let them catch me. I'd rather die than be tortured." She spun away from him and, before he could stop her, jumped over the edge of the several storeys high wall.

He didn't hesitate. He leapt after her, plummeting to the ground. He heard Marshall call his name as he grabbed hold of Brianne, his wings pumping the air as he tried to slow their descent. Both his wings and shoulders ached and he gritted his teeth as he tried to beat his wings harder. His grip on her hand slipped and she looked up at him, a plea in her eyes.

"Don't let go." The plea in his voice matched the one still in her eyes. He beat his wings as hard as possible, but it didn't seem enough. The ground came closer.

Brianne dropped her bundle. "Let go." She pulled away from him, the plea in her eyes becoming one of victory.

The moment she dropped, his descent slowed. "No." His heart leapt as she curled into a ball just before she hit the ground, rolling with the impact, coming up on her feet with a grin. The ground met him with a sharp jolt and he barely managed to remain on his feet.

Brianne grabbed her bundle and looking above them said, "Let's get out of here."

Talon looked upwards, seeing only one face watching him. Then something plummeted towards him and he jumped back. It was a belt pouch. He looked up again, but Marshall was gone.

"Come on, Talon. Do you want to be caught?"

Talon scooped up Marshall's belt pouch and ran after her.

Chapter Twenty-Five

Brianne

Brianne raced towards the mountains, her heart still pounding from her jump. It had been the biggest gamble of her entire life, but she hadn't had the time to argue with Talon. And he hadn't let her down, just like she wouldn't have let him die. She still couldn't believe instinct had made her step between him and Macklyn up on the wall. She glanced beside her as Talon reached her side.

"Where are we going?"

Brianne grinned at him. "How would I know? This is your land, not mine."

"Don't you ever do anything like that again or I'll let you fall."

"I was dead if I stayed."

Talon glanced away. "Come on. This way." He

headed left towards the forest that grew in the distance.

"Where are we going?"

"Probably on a one way trip to the Infernal World, but we might stop off at a lake on the way."

"We won't reach that forest if they decide to chase us down on horses." She had no idea what to do if that happened. There was no handy wall she could fling herself off. Not that she ever wanted to do that again. Those moments before Talon had caught her had been the longest seconds of her life.

"We're not going that far. Can you run any faster?"

"Not if we have to go too far a distance."

"We don't."

Brianne picked up her speed, unable to keep up with Talon. She glared at his back as her legs protested and her lungs burned. She was a fighter, not a runner. What was he thinking wearing them out like this? They needed to pace themselves so they could last longer. Then he disappeared, his wings retracting a moment before he vanished, followed by a sound that could have been a splash of water. Brianne slowed, wondering what had happened to him.

"Drop." Talon's voice came up from below the ground.

Brianne stopped at a large hole, unable to see what was in the darkness. "What's down there?"

"Does it matter? I survived it."

"What about the books I'm carrying? Will they survive it?"

"No, they'll get wet." There was a moment's silence. "Drop them down to me. I'll catch them."

Brianne stared at her bundle a moment before she made sure the shirt was tied around it securely. "Don't you dare let them get wet. I'm dropping them now."

"Hurry up."

Brianne dropped the bundle and waited. Not hearing a splash she hoped that was a good sign.

"I've got them and I'm out of the way. Your turn. The depth is about twice your height."

Brianne took a deep breath and jumped into the hole. Water rushed up to meet her and she kicked her legs, her arms dragging her back to the surface. Breaking through, she gasped for air, treading water as she tried to make out her surroundings. The pool of light from the hole did nothing to illuminate the area.

"Over this way."

Brianne swam towards Talon's voice. "I can't see anything."

"You don't need to, just swim past me. Once you

get in the water flow, let it carry you along. Tell me when you reach it and I'll join you."

Brianne felt the water tug at her. "I'm in it." She let the stream carry her along, treading water so she could stay afloat. He didn't answer her. "Talon?"

"Yes?"

"I was just checking you were still with me. How are those books?"

"Dry."

"Where is this taking us?"

"To a lake."

"Won't your people know to look for us there?"

"Yes, but we'll be faster than the horses."

"Where will we go?"

"I don't know."

Brianne felt frustration arrow through her at the lack of answers. They were running for their lives. They needed to figure out a plan and he wasn't being helpful.

"I thought you told me I couldn't fly."

Brianne frowned at the abrupt change in topic. "What?"

"Can I fly?"

She smiled. Was that still bothering him? "No."

"Then why did you jump?"

Her smile disappeared. "Because I hoped you'd catch me. It was better than letting them capture me."

"You expected me to catch you even though I can't fly."

Brianne couldn't resist laughing. "Yes, but you are good at dropping like a stone." She laughed again at his muttered reply. "Oh." Her gaze was drawn upwards. "What is it?" The entire ceiling of the cave flickered with lights.

"Bugs."

"Bugs." Brianne couldn't keep the disbelief from her voice. How could something so beautiful be created by a pest?

"Yes, bugs."

When they were past the bugs Brianne wanted to turn back and watch them, but she was worried she'd lose her sense of direction. "How much longer till we reach the lake?"

"Not long now."

"I'm freezing." She heard a sound in the distance, like a soft constant roar. Before she had a chance to ask what it was, Talon spoke.

"The water is a perfect temperature."

"If you're poisoned and suffering from a fever." She thought of her own poison she'd been taking, glad the berries had been left behind. It didn't matter if her usual colouring returned, everyone knew she wasn't a Tersten. What did matter was letting her people know about the Supreme One. "Talon?"

"Yes."

"I have to return to my people."

"No."

"Yes."

"My people need to be warned," Talon said.

"So do mine. Besides, who are you going to tell? Your father?"

"No. Our Political Leader."

"Who's that?"

"My mother."

Brianne tried to see him in the darkness. "You're joking, right?"

"No."

They were in so much trouble it was ridiculous. "We can't trust either of your parents."

"My mother would never sell out our people."

She bet he'd once thought that about his father. Before she had a chance to point that out, she was distracted by a light in the distance and the roaring sound getting louder. "What's that ahead?"

"A waterfall."

"What?"

Talon laughed. "It should be a breeze after falling from a wall."

"What about the books? You get them wet and I'm likely to push you off a wall after making sure your wings stay retracted."

"You do that and I'll take you with me." He paused. "Swim to the left. We don't actually go over the waterfall. We need to climb down beside it."

Brianne swam towards the bank she could now see from the light shining into the cave mouth. She swam past Talon, who struggled with the bundle he carried. Reaching the bank, she pulled herself out. Jumping to her feet, she ran alongside the river, calling out to him. "Throw them to me."

Talon stopped trying to swim long enough to toss the bundle to her. In those few moments he was swept out to the middle and Brianne raced along, watching as he tried to reach the bank. She placed the bundle well away from the edge and ran towards the waterfall. Lying on the bank, she reached out her arms as Talon was swept towards her, struggling to reach the edge.

"Talon!" She screamed his name, trying to be heard over the roar of the waterfall.

His gaze met hers as he tried to reach her. Then his

fingers grasped hers and within minutes he was lying on the bank beside her, gasping for breath. "Thanks."

"You probably could have released your wings and saved yourself."

Talon rolled onto his side to face her. He was silent for several minutes before he shook his head. "I have no idea how to release them right now."

Brianne reached out to him, her fingers touching his cheek and instantly drawing back from the heat. "Roll onto your stomach. Quickly." When he rolled without question she began to grow worried. Her worry became fear when she pressed her hands against his back and felt the heat of his skin. "Why didn't you say something? We should have got out of the water sooner."

"We couldn't have got out of the river any sooner. There's no bank until nearly the end." His words ended in a sharp indrawn breath.

"Sorry." She continued to work the muscles around the cramped ridges on his back. "You really need to rest. You've overdone things. What did you expect after never using your wings and then all of a sudden thinking you could fly?"

Talon swore, his hands becoming fists.

"You can scream if you want. No one would hear you over the waterfall." His wings sprung from his back and he turned enough to meet her gaze, his face drawn with pain.

"Yes, someone would."

There was no argument she could make. She too had been trained not to show weakness.

Chapter Twenty-Six

Talon

Talon staggered as they clambered out of the valley that the waterfall and lake nestled in, his clothes still damp after their trip along the river. His vision swam and he gritted his teeth as he tried to stay focused. A glance to the side showed Brianne kept pace with him, the books tied to her back.

"Do you want to stop and take a break?"

Talon shook his head, unable to speak.

Brianne sighed heavily. "Can we at least have a few minutes break? I can't keep up this pace."

He stared at her with narrowed eyes, trying to bring her expression into focus. It didn't help. The world and everything in it continued to swim around him. "A couple of minutes." He sat down, the words exhausting him a little more. He wasn't going to make it. Reaching for the belt pouch Marshall had given him, he untied it from the sleeves of his shirt that was still wrapped around his waist.

"Where did that come from?" Brianne asked.

Talon didn't bother answering. Staying conscious took enough of his concentration. He closed his eyes and felt around in the damp pouch. A small sheathed knife, a tin that he guessed contained flint and steel, a wet bandage and a small bottle that was probably antiseptic, and an oilskin wrapped parcel that felt like rations. All the usual contents of a soldier's belt pouch. He found only one difference. His fingers ran across an engraved ring and the piece of roughly cut bandage tied through it. Undoing the knot, he counted four knots until it was separated from the ring. Opening his eyes, he stared at the ring and bandage, trying to keep them from swimming in and out of focus.

"What does that mean?" Brianne asked.

"We need to change directions."

Brianne growled in frustration. "Can you tell me what's going on? We're meant to be in this together."

Talon stared at her, bringing her face into focus for a split second. Worry clouded her eyes and fatigue filled her face. He recalled those moments in the river when he'd thought he wasn't going to make it and she'd called out, her hands stretched towards him. Her grip when he reached for her and her determination not to let him go. As often as he tried to tell himself she was the enemy, he realised he no longer believed it. He didn't have a clue who the enemy was, but they needed to find out in a hurry.

"A message from Marshall. He's telling me where to meet him. He wants to help."

"How do we know it's not a trap?"

"We don't, but it's the only option we've got." As little as he wanted to admit it, he knew he couldn't keep pushing himself. They needed horses, food, supplies and somewhere to rest. Marshall had always stood by him, hopefully this time was no different. "We have to keep going." He struggled to his feet, squinting into the sky. It took him longer than it should have to get his bearings. "When we get to the top of the ridge, we head that way. We can't leave the trees, but we shouldn't have to. We'll eventually reach the foot of the mountains and there's a cave not far from there."

He forced himself to continue upwards, stumbling again. Then a shoulder was under his arm supporting him. He tried to pull away. She felt too fragile to take his weight.

"Don't be an idiot. We'll get there much faster if you cooperate."

He had little choice. The ground buckled beneath his feet and time became meaningless. Eventually, he realised they stood still, only the world moved around him, and Brianne peered up at him, repeating his name over and over.

"Talon."

"What?"

"Which way?"

"Huh?" He tried to focus on what she wanted.

"Which way." She spoke the words slowly.

They finally sank in and he looked around, trying to find something familiar. Half the day was gone and he had no idea how that had happened. Then he recognised where they were and stumbled forward. Again her shoulder was beneath his arm and they staggered onwards.

When they reached the cave, he didn't even have the strength to check for wild animals before he collapsed on the dirt, falling onto his face since his wings were still out. He felt gentle hands on his back and some of the pain eased. He fell into a deep sleep to be reluctantly jarred awake by a voice.

"You killed him!"

Talon struggled to sit up and reassure Marshall.

"He's fine. Or he was before you woke him with your shouting."

Talon would have grinned at the tone she used on Marshall if he'd had the energy. He felt her hands on him again, soothing and cool against his skin. He struggled to wake properly.

"Go back to sleep." Her tone was as gentle as her hands.

"Marshall," he croaked as he tried to focus on his friend.

"You should have trusted me."

"I've always trusted you, I just didn't want to get you killed because of me." Talon was finally able to take in his surroundings. A small fire, that was mostly glowing coals, was surrounded by rocks to block its flickering light from showing outside. Over it hung a skinned rabbit, the scent making his stomach rumble. He should have helped Brianne set up camp, not collapsed at her feet.

"Are you hungry?" Brianne asked.

Talon nodded.

"Sit over there and leave your wings out." She pointed to a large rock.

He recalled her comment about using stools to keep his wings out of the way and with a nod stumbled to the rock. "Sorry." He met Brianne's gaze as he sat down.

"For what? Preventing me from being smeared across the dirt at the foot of the wall? For getting us away from there? Or for leading us to this cave."

A wry smile escaped. "For passing out on you after I did all those things."

Brianne grinned. "Thanks for leaving me something to do. I wouldn't want to feel like I was some useless civilian."

Marshall interrupted them. "What's going on?"

"The Supreme One is an impostor," Brianne said.

"We don't know that," Talon argued.

Brianne took the rabbit from the fire and laid it on a flat rock. "Read the letters. He's an impostor. We're being manipulated by a country beyond the Feronian Mountains." She tore a leg from the rabbit and handed it to Talon.

He took the leg, shuffling it between his hands as he waited for it to cool. "Are you certain?"

"Where did you get the letters?" Marshall asked.

Brianne held out a couple of letters to Talon, waiting for him to wipe his hand against his trousers before he took them, then turned to Marshall. "The House of the Lord and Lady."

Marshall gaped at her. "You broke into a sacred building?"

"I wasn't the first. We were invaded centuries ago." She picked up a small slim book. "The diary of a true Elder talking about the real war. We all came from beyond the Feronian Mountains. We were two separate races working together and occasionally intermarrying. Our ancestors wanted to see what was on the other side of the mountains so they sent several battalions over to check, and if possible, set up an outpost. They were in the middle of building the fortress when two Elders came over the mountains. One went to the First Officer and said they must flee, the Terstens had killed all their people beyond the mountains and someone had been sent to tell them to kill off the rest. He brought the head of their leader to them, wrapped in a sack as proof. The other Elder told the General that the Caelians had tried to kill their people on the other side of the mountains and had failed, but they were to wipe out every last Caelian before they returned."

"Which Elder told the truth?" Talon asked.

"Neither. They weren't true Elders. They were Prilonians. The Elder who wrote this diary was imprisoned in the House, which had been newly built. The Prilonians tried to learn all the secrets of how the gods are worshipped so our ancestors didn't realise the Elders were actually the enemy."

"All the Holy Ones are Prilonians?" Marshall asked.

Talon swore when Brianne nodded. "What happens to our people who dedicate themselves to the gods?" He couldn't look at Marshall.

Brianne held his gaze for a moment before she reached for one of the letters. "This asks Elden to increase his efforts to encourage people to dedicate themselves to the gods as they need more slaves."

Marshall made a wounded sound and Talon had no idea what to say.

"What's wrong?" Brianne asked.

"My sister-" Marshall broke off.

"Last year," Talon said, and Brianne turned her gaze back to him. "She dedicated herself to the Lord and Lady last year." He watched as her expression hardened.

"We'll get her back, Marshall." Determination laced her voice, a promise of retribution added in.

"You can't promise me that," Marshall said.

"No, but I can promise to kill the man who made her a slave."

Marshall shook his head. "No, promise me instead that you'll help me be the one to kill him."

Brianne nodded. A single sharp nod. "Done." She

turned to Talon. "We have to return to my people. They would never knowingly help their enemy."

Talon longed to argue her words. How could his father have done this to them? "We should see my mother first." The look in her eyes promised him an argument. Feeling better than he had earlier, he looked forward to it.

Chapter Twenty-Seven

Brianne glared at Talon as they continued the argument they'd left unfinished when they went to sleep the previous night. Couldn't he see his family wasn't to be trusted?

Marshall interrupted their stand off. "I know where Warner is patrolling."

"Where?" Talon asked.

Brianne turned her glare on Marshall wishing she could tell him to stay out of their fight, but he still looked stunned from learning his sister was a slave. "What has Warner got to do with seeing your mother? Or not seeing her, which is the more sensible option."

Marshall kept his attention on Talon. "His unit's on the south patrol. If we left now we'd be able to catch them before they return to the city. He could take a message to your mother."

"I don't have anything I can use to write a message."

"You're going to get us killed." Brianne looked from one to the other, her glare still firmly in place. "If we're caught there'll be no one to warn my people. And why would he take a message to your mother and not your father?"

"Because Bellamy worships the ground my father walks on. Bellamy caused Warner to miss out on a unit captaincy so he could gain a rank instead."

"Warner is Bellamy's cousin which makes it worse," Marshall said.

Brianne met Talon's stare, recognising the determination in it. "Marshall delivers the message. You meet with your mother. We don't risk all three of us getting caught." She could see his hesitation and then he nodded. "There's a blank page in the back of that foreign book. You can use charcoal from the fire."

While Talon wrote his message, she hid the books and letters, keeping only the letter that talked of slaves in her belt pouch. Then, with the help of Marshall, she cleared away all evidence of their stay. The day had barely begun by the time they'd ridden the horses, Marshall had brought with him, to a place where they could watch Marshall give Warner the message.

Brianne sat in a tree on a branch near Talon, having climbed there on her own rather than risk his attempt at flying. She'd been surprised he'd managed to reach the branch near her on his first attempt. Not too far from them, on a well-worn path, Marshall sat on his horse, constantly looking around.

"What did you look like before you started taking vieteh berries?"

Brianne glanced at Talon, but his gaze remained on Marshall. "The same, just different colouring. It's starting to fade already."

"I noticed. Your eyes look odd. Patchy. What colour should they be?"

"Light blue."

"You do know vieteh berries are poisonous."

She shrugged. "I was under a death sentence anyway."

Talon looked over at her. "Because you had no wings?"

"Yes, but my family arranged other options for me."

"Being a spy?"

Brianne shook her head. "Teaching fledglings or joining the House."

"Becoming a slave."

Her gaze was drawn to Marshall. "They didn't know." She thought of Talon's family and how his father had known about the Prilonians. No, her family would never sell her into slavery, but her grandfather and uncle had never planned to let her join the House. Marshall drew himself upright and she turned to see where he looked. Ten soldiers rode towards him on horseback, weapons at the ready.

Brianne's hand rested over the throwing darts in their leather case on her belt. She didn't trust Marshall and she certainly didn't trust the soldiers.

"Warner," Marshall called out. "I have a message for you to take to the Political Leader."

The soldiers halted and one moved slightly ahead of the others, still leaving plenty of distance between him and Marshall. "Why can't you take it to her?"

"I found Talon. I need you to let his mother know."

Warner shook his head. "He's a traitor. It's death for anyone who helps him."

"He has information proving the General and Bellamy are traitors. I've talked him into giving the information to his mother, even though he doesn't think she'll believe him. I think she will. Talon will meet with her if you can get this message to her in time." Marshall held up the letter.

"What makes you think she'll listen?" one of the other soldiers asked.

"Because of the proof. She'll have to do something about it or the General will destroy our people. He's negotiating with people beyond the Feronian Mountains, but he's ignoring the fact they're going to turn on us in the long run." Marshall used the excuse they'd decided on.

"And this proof shows Bellamy to be a traitor too?" Warner asked.

Marshall nodded. "He's been the General's errand boy, delivering messages."

Warner rode forward. "I can't promise anything other than to give the letter to the Political Leader."

"Don't do it, Warner. What if you're charged with helping Talon? It's death," one of the other soldiers said.

"I'm not helping him. I'm letting the Political Leader know some important information. It's up to her to decide what's to be done with it." Warner took the letter and tucked it into his belt pouch.

Marshall's next words were too quiet for Brianne to hear and she tried to read his lips, unable to figure out the words. Was he betraying them? Then Marshall rode away, the soldiers rode on and Talon started to climb out of the tree.

Brianne waited a moment longer, watching to make sure the soldiers didn't double back. She clambered out of the tree and strode after Talon, who walked towards the horses.

When Marshall joined them, Brianne asked, "What did you say to Warner when he took the letter?"

"To tell his friend not to join the House. Wait a while before he makes the decision."

Brianne nodded. "Do you think he'll listen?"

Marshall shrugged. "I don't know. I can only hope."

Chapter Twenty-Eight

Talon

Talon tried to remain still. He wanted to pace and every sound had him fighting the urge to draw his sword. His mother would be joining him any minute and he didn't think it'd be a good idea to greet her with a drawn sword. Maybe if they'd made the meeting time earlier he wouldn't be feeling so impatient, but he had needed to give her enough time to get the message.

He glanced around the clearing, making sure he didn't stare too long in the direction Brianne and Marshall were hidden. His back tightened and he ignored the urge to set his wings free. Having his wings out would probably be as good an idea as greeting his mother with a sword. A sound drew his attention and he turned to see his mother ride into the clearing, dismounting near him.

"Do you realise the trouble you've caused?" Larena asked.

Instead of answering, he held out the letter they'd gone back to the cave to fetch.

She didn't take it. "What is this?"

"A letter from my father to the Supreme One, who he addresses as Elden, begging for extra time to pay the tribute when we had that late harvest a couple of years ago."

"The Supreme One has no other name than Holy Father."

Talon shook the letter at her. "Read it. Just read it. Tell me this isn't my father's handwriting."

Larena took the letter from him and opened it.

Talon waited as she read, wanting to tell her to hurry up. He remained quiet, trying to stay calm. The meeting wasn't going exactly how he'd expected.

Larena finally raised her head. "Who else knows of this? Marshall? The Caelian girl?"

Something didn't feel right to him. "Only I've read it. I wanted to show you before anyone else saw it."

"Where are they? Marshall and the girl?"

What did it matter where they were? Especially Marshall. "Once I agreed to meet with you Marshall said he was going back to his unit. And the Caelian girl," Talon shrugged, "I don't know where she is."

"Good." Larena nodded. She placed the letter in her belt pouch and raised her right hand. "I once had great hopes for you." Disappointment filled her voice.

Talon looked behind her to where a unit of soldiers rode towards him led by Bellamy, his father bringing up the rear. "Why?" Pain hit him. This time an ache in his heart rather than his wings.

"You have no idea what you nearly did. You could have destroyed Terst." She stepped away from him. "Take him."

Bellamy dismounted, coming towards Talon with a grin. "It'll be my pleasure, ma'am."

His first urge was to fight, but then he thought of Marshall and Brianne watching him. Marshall would never let him fight alone. He wasn't certain about Brianne, not after she'd warned him against this. "I'll come quietly. I have no wish to hurt my own people." The last words were said with a pointed look towards his father. He managed to refrain from saying, unlike some.

As soon as Talon was mounted behind a soldier, his hands tied behind him, they headed to the city. He was put in a cell beneath the fortress and his father stood at the barred doorway, a look of disappointment on his face.

"Why?" Talon grabbed hold of a bar, his hands now untied.

"Sometimes it's better to bow your head than to lose it."

Talon stared at his father, hardly able to believe the words he'd spoken. "No. Never."

"Then you wouldn't have made a good general. I have to make the decisions that are for the greater good. Sometimes you need to sacrifice a few so the majority survive."

Bitterness twisted through Talon. "I never would have made a good general, not with my wings."

"You should have come to me. The Prilonians can remove them without killing the patient now."

Disbelief arrowed through Talon. Letting go of the bars, he took a step backwards. "Who are you?"

"I could say the same." Footsteps echoed down the corridor and Barrett turned towards them. "Elden."

Elden came into Talon's view, his black robed figure stopping to face him, his features still hidden by the hood of his robe. A million questions came to mind, but he didn't have a clue which one he should ask first.

After a moment, Elden turned to Barrett. "You

can't be seen down here. It doesn't look good. You need to disassociate yourself from this mess." He made a waving motion towards Talon.

"I'm not a mess, I'm his son." Talon stepped forward to grab a hold of the bars again.

Barrett nodded. "You're right. I'll leave it in your hands."

Talon stared after his father. He couldn't believe he was walking off without a single word to his only son. "Father!" No reply. His father kept walking until he was out of sight, the sound of his footsteps fading into the distance his only answer. It was a nightmare. He'd always known his father was a hard man, but to desert his own family? He would have sworn it was an impossibility.

Elden laughed. "You didn't really think he'd go against me to save you, did you?"

"Why would he help you? What did you promise him?"

"His enemy dead and a powerful ally."

"How long ago did he make this bargain?"

"Years ago. When he first became general. I showed him what he faced if he went against us."

Talon stared at Elden, wishing he could tear the hood from his face to see the man who would destroy them all. He finally knew which question he needed answered, the one that would answer all his other questions. "Are you ever going to help my people defeat the Caelians?"

"You are warriors. What would you be without the Caelians to fight?" His words hung in the air a moment before he added. "What would you *do* if you didn't have them to fight?" He turned and strode away.

"No!" Talon's hands tightened around the bars. Brianne had been right. Elden had no plan to help his people win. He wanted to keep them in a futile war forever. Pushing away from the bars he started to pace. What had he done? He hoped Brianne managed to get the books and letters to her people. Hoped the Caelians hadn't gone crawling to their enemy in a desperate attempt to save their people.

Pain tore across his back and he ripped his shirt off, setting his wings free. He was dead anyway, why should he care who saw his wings?

Chapter Twenty-Nine

Brianne struggled to hold Marshall back. "You can't help him." She slammed him against the tree he'd jumped out of when they'd seen Talon captured.

"I have to try." Marshall tried to break away from her.

They landed on the ground, sticks and small rocks digging into her body. "Not like this. You'll throw your life away." If there was anything she could have used, she would have hit him over the head and knocked him out.

"They'll kill him."

"Not right away. We'll have time to save him." Relief filled her when Marshall stilled. He'd broken her hold so many times it was only that she was quicker than him that he hadn't escaped.

"When?"

"We need to find out where he's been taken and how to get in. Do you know anyone else who'll be able to help?"

"No one. They'd be worried about being executed too."

"If I let you go, will you promise not to go after Talon until we have a plan?" She continued to watch him for a moment after he nodded. She guessed she couldn't hold him down all day. He'd break her hold eventually. Letting him go, she rose to her feet, dusting herself off.

"There's no way to get him out of the fortress. No one can get in or out of it."

Brianne grinned. "I got in."

Marshall stared at her a moment before he finally smiled. "Maybe, but even you won't be able to do it twice."

She thought of Garnet who'd believed in her. Garnet who adored her older brother. "I need to get a message to someone."

"Who?"

"Garnet."

Marshall shook his head. "Talon would kill us if we involved her in any way."

"If we don't get help, Talon won't have a chance to kill us, he'll be dead."

"I don't know how we're going to get a message to her. She spends a lot of time in the fortress. She only goes into the city a couple of times a week."

Brianne frowned. "Where in the fortress?"

"Huh?"

"Where does she spend most of her time?"

Marshall shrugged. "At her home, in her room or visiting friends who also live in the fortress."

She tried to think of Garnet's room. There had been a window looking out over the wall to the mountains. "Can you get me a bow?"

"No." Marshall shook his head. "But you can borrow my crossbow. Why?"

"That will do."

It took some convincing, but Marshall finally agreed to help her. At nightfall they found themselves at the foot of the wall, Marshall's crossbow at Brianne's back and a length of rope tied around her waist, as they waited for a patrol to pass by on the top of the wall.

Marshall ran his hand over the stone wall. "This isn't going to work."

"I've climbed worse. Not to mention taller."

Brianne tucked her fingers into the gaps between the large stones.

"You're going to get yourself killed," Marshall said.

Brianne laughed softly as she wondered if Talon had found it as annoying when she'd told him the same. "Don't get yourself caught and let me know if you see any patrols on top of the wall above me." She reached for a higher handhold, the action familiar.

Marshall moved away from the wall, muttering about idiotic plans.

When she eventually reached the top, she pulled herself onto the wall, dropping lightly to a crouch as she scanned the area. It was all clear. She crossed to the other side of the wall and searched for the correct window as she readied the crossbow, a note through the head of the bolt. A deep breath to steady herself and then she let it out as she shot the bolt into the room, aiming for the ceiling so she didn't accidentally hurt Garnet if she was in there. She was relieved the shot was perfect. Spending a couple of hours practising that afternoon with the crossbow had obviously been a good idea.

It seemed forever before a figure appeared at the window, holding a lantern. Brianne stood up and waved, grinning when Garnet bounced around at the window. She waved Garnet out of the way and when the window was clear, shot another bolt over, one end of the rope tied to it. She returned the crossbow to her back while she waited for Garnet to tie the rope securely. Several minutes later, she was at the window again, waving Brianne over.

With one end of the rope still tied to her, Brianne climbed onto the edge of the wall. She eyed the distance, wincing. This was going to hurt. Jumping, she aimed for the wall of the fortress with her legs, running across the wall to take some of the momentum and impact out of the jump. Pushing away from the wall, she let herself swing back under the window, her shoulder banging against the wall. For one moment she thought the rope was going to let go, then she was dangling at the end of the rope listening. Everything was quiet. No one had seen her. Grabbing hold of the rope, she started to pull herself upwards. It was quicker than looking for handholds in the wall and she was soon dragging herself into the bedroom.

Garnet threw her arms around Brianne. "I can't believe you jumped across like that. For a minute I thought you were dead. You even dragged my bed across to the window. I didn't think it would move when I tied the rope to it."

Untying herself, Brianne glanced around, taking note of the heavy timber bed. "Is anyone else home?"

Garnet shook her head. "Things are crazy here. There's constant arguments and some people want to know what Talon found that made him think our father is a traitor."

"Where are they keeping him?"

"In the cells beneath the fortress. There's no way we can get him out of there."

Brianne grinned. "People keep telling me that, but here I am after being told getting in here a second time was impossible."

Garnet grabbed hold of Brianne's hands. "Do you think you can get him out?"

"I hope so, but I'm going to need some help."

"I knew you were our friend, even when everyone kept telling me you're a spy."

"I am a spy, Garnet."

"But you're helping Talon."

She nodded, still not quite sure why she was, but the thought of leaving him behind hadn't been acceptable. "Tell me everything about the cells and how to get there."

Chapter Thirty

Talon rose to his feet when he heard footsteps coming towards his cell. He was at the bars immediately. "Garnet. What are you doing here?"

Garnet glanced towards the guard at her side. "He let me come and say goodbye." She reached through the bars for his hand. "I don't want you to die. They're talking about hanging you tomorrow."

He tried to keep his expression neutral, determined to keep Garnet safe. "Everything will be fine. You stay out of this mess and look after yourself." Talon gripped her hand.

Garnet wrapped her other hand around their clasped hands. "I went to our father's office looking for him, but I couldn't find him."

Talon frowned as he felt her press something small

and metallic into his hand. "You know you're not meant to go in his office when he's not in there, Garnet."

"And he wasn't in his room."

"Don't go wandering around. Stay in your room until all this is over." Why was she telling him this?

"Come on, Miss. You only wanted a few minutes to say goodbye. Time's up."

Still holding onto Talon's hand, Garnet turned her face to the guard. "Can you open the cell so I can hug him goodbye? Please?"

The guard shook his head. "Come now. Your goodbyes are done."

Garnet turned back to Talon, reaching through with a hand to pull him close and whisper in his ear. "Brianne's waiting for you. I stole the key from our father's room. I'll try to keep the guard busy, you knock him out." She pulled away, head bowed as she walked away, the guard following.

Talon stared after her until she was out of sight before he opened his hand to see a key. Dread pooled in his stomach. Their father would know who'd taken the key. He had to get Garnet out of the fortress. Opening the cell door, he carefully swung it open, running lightly down the corridor. The guard started to turn, but he didn't have a chance. Talon smashed him into the stone wall. Hard enough to knock him out. The guard was going to have a massive headache when he came to.

Garnet gasped, staring down at the guard. "Is he alive?"

Talon nodded. "Where's Brianne?"

"Are you sure?"

"Yes. Now where's Brianne?"

"This way."

Talon ran after Garnet who sprinted down the empty corridors. "Where are all the guards?"

"Brianne took care of them."

Garnet's earlier question made him worry for his people. "Are they alive?"

Garnet came to a stop in front of a door and nodded. She tapped lightly, then tapped again. The door swung open and Brianne stood there. She grinned when she saw Talon, her grin fading when he glared at her.

"What did you think you were doing getting my sister mixed up in this mess?"

"That she was better off out of it than stuck here with your traitorous family." She paused. "Think you can fly?"

Talon was torn between wanting to agree with her and wanting to keep his sister completely out of it, but that was impossible as long as she was at the fortress. "Let's hope so."

With a single sharp nod, Brianne stepped into the corridor. "This way then." She led them up a couple of flights of stairs, each time sending Garnet first to check for guards. Then she was entering an empty room, flinging open the window.

"Get Garnet over the wall. Marshall is waiting for you on the other side of the wall, behind Garnet's room."

Talon stared at Brianne. Surely she didn't expect him to leave her in here, not after she'd rescued him. That didn't make sense. "What about you?"

Brianne picked up a familiar rope tied to a large stick. She grinned at him. "You better come back for me. I'll be at the base of the wall." Flinging the rope out the window, she checked the stick was secure before she lowered herself over the window ledge.

Talon waited until she'd cleared the ledge before he climbed out, clinging to the window frame as he stretched his wings. "Wrap your arms around me, Garnet, and hold on tight." As soon as she clung to him, he dropped backwards, pumping his wings hard so they immediately rose into the air. When they were above the height of the wall, he struggled to make his wings tilt. It took far longer than he liked, but he was finally across the wall and lowered them to the ground.

They landed in a tangle of limbs and Talon rolled away, coming to his feet as movement caught his attention. He relaxed slightly when Marshall called out his name. Helping Garnet to her feet, he pushed her into Marshall's arms. "Get her out of here. I'll meet you at the cave."

"Where's Brianne?" Marshall demanded.

"I've got to go back for her." He launched into the air, the action feeling more familiar, but once again, tilting his wings to be able to fly across the top of the wall was an effort. He headed for the ground, scanning the area for Brianne. When she called out, he dropped rapidly, flying towards her.

"Took your time, didn't you?" The two soldiers, that she kept at bay with her sword, turned towards him. She used his distraction to barrel into them, knocking one to the ground, throwing the other off balance before she ran to Talon.

He reached out for her as he began to pump his wings, sending them into the sky with only a tenuous hold on Brianne. "Don't let go."

She clung with one arm, the other still holding a sword. "Get us to the wall. We can set down up there."

The wall was filled with running feet and many shouts as Brianne began to slip from his arms. "Drop your sword and hold on tight," Talon said.

They were over the other side of the wall and Brianne laughed wryly. "No way, I'd probably land on the sword. Drop faster. Pull up hard at the end."

He tried to follow her directions, but she hadn't said how fast. The speed of their fall dragged her from him. Fear filled him. He reached for her shadowy figure in the dark, missed, then finally caught her arm as he tried to pull up hard. It wasn't enough. They were slammed into the ground, the wind knocked out of them.

Brianne was the first to speak, groaning as she struggled to rise. "When are you going to learn how to fly?"

"Where's that infernal sword?"

"That way. I threw it from us when we were close to the ground."

"Which way?" If she'd pointed out the direction, he hadn't noticed in the darkness.

Brianne moved away from him. "I've got it. Where's Marshall and Garnet?"

"I sent them to the cave."

"Come on then. Our horses are tied up over here."

He followed the sound of her footsteps, the world

full of shadows. He had no idea how they were going to find their way to the cave in the dark. The only upside was that it'd make it difficult for pursuers to follow.

Chapter Thirty-One

Brianne stared at the letter she'd just finished reading by the campfire where their breakfast of wild foul baked in the coals. She looked over to Marshall and Talon who'd returned to arguing after the few hours sleep they'd managed to have after rescuing Talon. Beyond them, Garnet was curled up in a bed of leaves, the embroidered shirt rolled up for a pillow, while she read the Elder's diary.

"Talon." She waited until he looked over from his argument. "Listen to this." She paused before she read out the section of the letter. "We are sending more soldiers to protect the mountain passes as the rebels have increased their attempts at crossing into Terst." She looked up from the letter.

"What does it say next?" Talon asked.

"Just tells Elden which garrisons to send the extra tribute to." She glanced at the top of the letter. "It was written nearly a year ago. The House asked for a larger share of the crops to cover the rise in followers. I remember it because Grandad complained how they were already well fed and the army deserved more rations than the Holy Ones."

"We have to give the House a portion of every harvest. My grandparents own an orchard and they always send part of each harvest there," Marshall said.

"You're missing the point," Brianne said.

"Which is what?" Marshall asked.

"The rebels," Talon answered before Brianne had a chance.

She nodded. "Yes. There are other people fighting the Prilonians."

"How do we find them?" Marshall asked.

"We take out the garrisons and let them find us," Talon said.

"Exactly. But first we let my people know because we need help," Brianne said.

"There are Terstens who'd fight if they knew what was going on," Marshall said.

"Where?" Brianne asked.

Garnet sat up, setting the diary aside. "There are

people who argue against every decision my parents make. They'd love to see them fail."

"But that doesn't mean they'll fight against the Prilonians." Talon glared at Marshall.

"Some of them would," Marshall said.

Brianne decided she better interrupt before they began a new argument. Talon was probably going to be annoyed with Marshall for a very long time for helping her involve Garnet. "Would you know who to talk to?" When Marshall nodded, she kept her gaze on him, determined not to let Talon sway her. "You and Garnet find them while Talon and I go to my people."

"No."

Brianne ignored Talon. "Only take a couple of the letters. Ones in Barrett's handwriting so they know they're true."

"She's not helping," Talon said.

"I'm not a little kid." Garnet's eyes narrowed as she turned her gaze on her brother. "I can do this."

Continuing to ignore Talon, Brianne kept her gaze on Marshall. "We have to keep this place safe. We need somewhere to meet up when we all return. Don't show it to anyone you don't trust."

Remaining seated, Talon reached out to Brianne,

grasping her shoulder and turning her to face him. "You're not endangering my sister."

Brianne met his gaze, not at all surprised by the anger she saw. "What would you have her do instead? Sit by and let them steal her country? Have all her friends taken as slaves? Why shouldn't she fight for her world? Would you sit back and let someone take everything from you?"

"No, but she's only a kid."

"I'm not a kid," Garnet protested.

Brianne ignored Garnet. "So, because she's a kid she should let them take everything from her?"

"No!" The word exploded from Talon.

"Then what should she do?" She watched as Talon wrestled with the question.

Swearing, he rose to his feet and stalked away.

Brianne hesitated only a moment before she followed him outside. The horizon was tinged with colour from the rising sun and Talon stood with his back to her, his wings out. She came to a stop beside him.

"I don't want anything to happen to her."

Brianne could make no promises.

Talon turned towards her. "Garnet and Marshall are all I have left."

She reached out and clasped his hand, meeting his gaze. "No they're not."

Talon's gaze lowered to their clasped hands as he remained silent for several minutes. He finally raised his gaze and met hers. "We should leave soon, before the day is too far advanced."

"Garnet can help?"

Talon nodded. "Yes."

Garnet shrieked from the mouth of the cave, running out to throw herself at her brother, breaking Brianne's grip on him. "Thank you, thank you, thank you."

Talon held her from him, his expression stern. "You'll be careful."

"Of course."

Marshall joined them. "I'll look out for her."

"Both of you be careful." Talon looked from one to the other.

Brianne headed for the cave, pausing at the entrance. "I'm taking the diary and a couple of letters. Hide the rest once you choose which letters you're taking."

Garnet ran after her. "But I haven't finished reading it yet."

Chapter Thirty-Two

Talon

Talon sat on his horse, waiting for Brianne to rejoin him. Yesterday had been spent avoiding patrol units and the last thing he'd wanted to do was spend time going out of their way so she could pick up a couple of things. And how long did she need? Maybe he should go after her. What if she'd got into trouble?

His gaze searched the area. How was he meant to see the enemy? Rock pillars rose randomly throughout the wide gully that narrowed at one end, red dust in every direction he looked. He missed the open meadows of his country where you could see an enemy from miles away.

Brianne stepped around a rock pillar, wearing fitted trousers, a vest like top and sleek boots. A bow hung at her back. These clothes suited her a lot more than the serviceable ones worn by Tersten soldiers.

"Why were your things in the middle of nowhere?"

"Because I didn't trust Macklyn to take them home for me." She put her other gear in the saddlebags, tying the Tersten boots on behind the saddle before she mounted.

"He didn't look like he could be trusted." In fact, he'd reminded him of Bellamy, always out for himself. "Which way now?" He glanced around. How did Caelians put up with all this red dust? He was sick of it.

Brianne nudged her horse forward. "This way."

"How much longer?"

"We'll get there late afternoon, but we should wait until dark. I don't want anyone knowing we've arrived, especially not the Prilonians. Elden may have sent word to look out for us."

Talon nodded as he rode beside her. Another look around showed more red dust. Where were the trees, the rich earth and the lakes? It was a wonder they could raise any crops on ground like this.

The land they rode through didn't change and by late afternoon they saw the fortified city in the distance. Towers rose high above the walls, making it look like many fingers reaching for the sky, a multi-towered castle behind them.

"Why are the buildings so tall? It must take forever to reach the top."

"Not if you have wings. For many of the towers that's the only way you can enter them."

"What about people without wings?"

"There are no people without wings, only children. They're easily carried by their parents."

"How do we get in?" Talon began to think she wasn't going to answer, but she finally faced him.

"I can get us in on foot, but you'll have to fly us to my grandfather's home. I'll get us to the base and it'll be straight up from there." She paused. "Think you can fly yet?" Her lips curved into a smile, a challenge in her eyes.

"Of course I can." He was getting better at it all the time. He'd be outflying Macklyn before long.

Brianne grinned. "I guess I'll soon see for myself."

They left their horses tied to a narrow rock pillar, in a well hidden gully, and headed for the city once it was dark. Talon followed Brianne as she glided from shadow to shadow, his wings still out. Having them out more often and regularly doing the exercises Brianne had taught him seemed to be lessening the pain. His fever had also gone, which was good since

Caelis was warmer with its lack of shady trees and grassy meadows.

The wall around the city was made from the same stones used in Terst, as were the towers, but that was the only similarity. The streets were deserted, there were very few lowset buildings and his gaze was drawn upwards to where Caelians flew overhead. Each time someone passed he tensed, ready to draw his sword should one of them swoop down on them.

Brianne stopped at the foot of a tower that shot up into the sky. Towards the top, a small platform jutted out. "Are you ready?"

Talon continued to stare at the platform, highlighted by moonlight. "You want me to land on that?"

"Think you can do it?"

Talon hesitated. What choice did they have? "Yes."

"There'll be a guard up there. Try not to land on him."

"Three of us are meant to fit up there?" Surely she didn't really mean that.

"If you can't do it, let me know and I'll climb up, but it'll take me hours and someone's likely to notice. Especially since it's something only a dirt walker would do."

He heard the derision in her voice when she said

the words 'dirt walker'. It reminded him of the way Macklyn had said them. What would it have been like not to be able to hide how different you were from everyone else? "I can do this. Are you ready?"

Instead of answering, she removed her bow from her back and leaned against his chest, holding her arms out slightly, an arrow in the other hand.

Talon wrapped his arms around her chest, his hands gripping her shoulders. "What are you planning? You're not going to shoot the guard, are you?"

"I hope not." She paused. "Fly."

Talon launched into the air, holding Brianne tight. The platform came closer. When he was beside it, he started to tilt his wings.

The guard raised his bow, an arrow trained on them. "Move away."

Brianne raised her own bow and called out at the same time, "It's Brianne Devin, I need to see my grandfather."

"Who's with you?" The guard's bow remained trained on them.

Talon struggled to keep his height constant while he inched slowly towards the platform, his wings barely tilting.

"I need to see my grandfather. It's important."

"Can we land?" Talon whispered in her ear. If she said no, he didn't think he could keep hovering.

The door swung open. "What's going on out here?"

"Grandad."

"Brianne. What are you doing here? Macklyn said you'd been caught."

"Can we land?" Talon asked Brianne again.

"I brought someone for you to meet," Brianne said.

Talon watched as the old man made a sharp motion and the guard lowered his bow. Taking that as an invitation, he slowly dropped to the platform, relieved when he managed to stay on his feet.

Holding the door open, the old man stepped out of the way. "Inside, quickly."

Talon let go of Brianne as she pulled away from him, staying close to her side as he looked around. The guard stayed outside and Brianne followed her grandfather to a lantern lit room with a desk, two stools on the side closest to them, a single stool on the far side.

Once the door was closed, the old man turned to Talon. "Who are you?" His gaze was drawn to the dark feathers.

With a grin, Brianne stepped forward and answered before Talon could. "This is Talon Morin,

General Barrett Morin's son. Talon, meet my grandfather, Briant Finnin."

Chapter Thirty-Three

Brianne

Brianne paced the floor while her uncle finished reading the letters she'd brought and her grandfather skimmed through the diary. Talon stood in a corner, his wings still out and his expression wary. With the length of time it was taking the two of them to go over the information they'd brought, she and Talon could have collected the horses themselves instead of letting Briant send someone for them. It would have been a lot more interesting than being cooped up in her grandfather's office.

Ewyn nudged Briant, who was seated on a stool next to him. Briant looked at the letter Ewyn read, then almost as one they both glanced at Brianne.

She stopped pacing. "What?"

"Go back to your pacing and let us finish reading," Briant said.

Brianne strode forward, planting her hands on the desk. "What did you just read?" When her relatives looked past her, she turned to see Talon standing at her shoulder, his hands at his sides, one hovering at the hilt of his sword. She faced her relatives. "Well?"

Briant shared a look with Ewyn before he rummaged in his desk drawer, rose from the stool and handed her a folded piece of paper. "You're welcome to use my living room if you want some privacy to read it."

Brianne's hands remained planted on the desk, her gaze meeting Briant's. "Who is it from?"

"Zinervie."

Brianne recoiled, as if struck, her back pressing against Talon's chest. She felt his hand at her side, steadying her. "For me." The words sounded more statement than question, but Brianne didn't think she could have heard correctly.

"Go into the living room and read it. Give Ewyn time to finish the letters." Briant continued to hold the letter out.

It was Talon who took the letter and tugged on her arm, drawing her from the room. She didn't even know if she wanted to read it. Sitting on one of the cushioned, backless rectangular seats, she warily eyed the letter Talon held.

Talon sat down beside her. "Do you want me to read it for you?"

Brianne shook her head, taking the letter from him. Whatever it was, she'd face it, not cower behind someone else. It was several minutes before she could open it and several more before the words started to make sense. She looked up at Talon, dropping the letter to her lap, shaking her head.

"What does it say?"

She looked away from him, taking a deep breath. "I'm going to kill Macklyn." Rising to her feet, she started to stride towards the entrance only to be captured by Talon.

"What did it say?"

"Let me go." She struggled against him.

"Tell me and I might even help you."

She stopped fighting, his arms still around her, and met his gaze. Brown eyes stared at her, concern in their depths. "He told Zinervie that I'd decided to join the House. That after days of contemplation at the town where I was staying, I finally figured out that I wanted to forget my past and live only for the Lord and Lady, who accept everyone, even abominations."

She fell silent, unable to find the words to tell him the rest.

"What happened?" His voice was soft.

Time spun out as she continued to stare up at him. "He told my Uncle I was discovered and captured. They put about the story that I was captured during a raid on the town I was staying at and presumed dead." Her voice faltered and Talon's arms tightened around her. She lowered her gaze, seeing only the golden brown of his skin. When she finally managed to continue, her voice was a whisper. "She joined the House in my memory and sent a letter to my grandfather apologising to him for not being a better friend to me while I was alive."

"I'll help you kill him." Talon pressed her head against his chest.

She rested there for a moment before she pulled away and headed back to her grandfather. Stepping into the room, she was about to ask where Macklyn was, when she noticed her grandfather was alone. "Where's Uncle Ewyn?"

"Questioning Macklyn. We thought it might be best that we take him into custody before you decided to kill him."

Brianne glared at her grandfather. Sometimes it

was annoying how well he knew her. "He doesn't deserve to live."

"Maybe not, but we need to know why he told us you'd been captured."

"I bet I could get the information out of him before he dies." She thought of the knife in her boot, the one Macklyn didn't think she could use. She'd show him how well she could use it.

"No." Briant shook his head. "Forget about Macklyn for a minute, I want to talk to you about the garrisons."

"What about Zinervie?"

"She left yesterday."

"Left?"

"With two other new penitents. Left to go into seclusion for training to become a penitent."

Brianne dropped onto the stool. "They've taken her away already?"

Briant nodded.

She felt Talon's hand rest on her shoulder and placed one of her own on his. "We have to find them."

"Ewyn is organising aerial searches. By morning this city will be locked down. Only those with wings will be able to get in or out," Briant said.

"Why?"

"So that when we raid the House of the Lord and Lady and the earthly dwelling of the Master of the Infernal World none can escape."

She felt Talon's hand tighten on her shoulder. "I want to help."

"So do I," Talon said.

Chapter Thirty-Four

Talon

Talon stood beside Brianne as they waited with a group of soldiers for the word to attack. His sword was still sheathed, but he was ready to draw it, his hand resting on the hilt. Around him stood men and women with wings at rest, all wearing one of the backless vests like he'd been given. It had taken less time than he'd expected to gather the soldiers and get them into position for the attack, less than an hour, impressing him with how well organised the Caelian army was.

The moment the call went out he drew his sword, looking forward to his first battle in years. He raced forward with the soldiers attacking on foot, the aerial squads already above with bows drawn. Swinging his sword at the Prilonian that attacked him, Talon quickly disarmed the robed figure, hitting him over the head so he crumpled to the ground. A Caelian came forward and tied him up. Talon looked around, seeing three Prilonians attacking a single Caelian. He ran forward. The moment he attacked, the Prilonian dropped the sword he'd wielded inexpertly and grovelled at his feet, begging for mercy.

Talon looked at the Prilonian in disgust. It would have been far easier to kill the man than tie him up, but he had his orders. Once the man was tied, he raced back into the fight. Seeing Brianne attacking a brown robed figure, he moved in to help her. Between the two of them they made short work of him. Brianne gave him a grin before she dashed back into the fighting, leaving him to secure their prisoner.

Roughly tying up his prisoner, he growled, "You're lucky I don't kill you."

"You'll wish you had when word gets out about what's happened here tonight." The man's hood had fallen back to reveal light brown hair and bluish green eyes.

"The city has been locked down. No one gets past the walls tonight," Talon said.

The man laughed.

Talon grabbed him by a fistful of robe, pulling him close. "Tell me."

"Killing me won't give you the answer you need."

Brianne joined him. "What's wrong?"

"He reckons a message is going to get out about the attack." Talon continued to hold the man's robe.

"I wonder if they've finished torturing Macklyn and are ready for another one." Brianne looked the man up and down. "I bet they could have the information out of him in two minutes. I've been told the longest anyone can last is ten minutes, but I'm not sure that counts since he was insane by the end."

"You lie," the man said.

Brianne slowly smiled. "Do I?"

Not knowing if she spoke the truth or not, Talon decided to help her efforts. "I was there when Briant ordered Macklyn tortured to find out what he knew. If he's willing to order the torture of one of his own I doubt he'd worry about ordering his enemy tortured."

Brianne drew her curved knife and held it out to Talon. "How about you start on him while I organise having him collected by some guards."

Talon took the knife and eyed the man up and down. "Where do you reckon I should start? How about the fingers of his right hand?"

"There's a tunnel," the man blurted out.

"Where?" Talon pressed the knife to the man's cheek.

"Below. At the end of the southern corridor. It's locked. You won't be able to stop him."

"Where's the key?"

"The messenger has it."

Talon let the man drop, handing the dagger back to Brianne. "We need to try."

She nodded. "Give me a minute." She ran to the closest soldier, told him something, then ran back to Talon. "Let's go."

Talon led the way to the altar, heading into the room behind it and down the stairs. When they reached the bottom of the stairs, he turned to Brianne. "Which way is south?"

She flung a door open. "This way."

He followed her, glad of the lanterns that hung above them along the corridor. They were part way along when two robed figures burst from one of the doors, swinging swords.

Talon's sword met one of the blades, Brianne fighting at his side, protecting him from the other. There was barely enough room to fight in the corridor and he swung fiercely, driving his opponent back into the room he'd come from. Soldiers appeared at his side, telling him to go.

"Come on," Brianne called out, the robed figure she'd been fighting now subdued by two of the soldiers. She didn't wait, dashing into the corridor ahead of him.

Sheathing his sword, Talon ran after her, finding a soldier at her side carrying a large axe. He ran behind the two of them, until they reached the far end of the corridor, a closed door in front of them. Moving forward, Talon tried to open it. "Locked."

"Stand back," the soldier with the axe ordered.

Talon stepped away as the soldier swung the axe at the wooden door. He turned to Brianne. "What made you think of the axe?"

"I didn't. I said we needed something to break down a locked door."

Talon grinned at her. "That should do it."

With a loud crack, the door burst open to show an unlit corridor. The soldier gestured inside. "After you."

Brianne grabbed a lantern from a ceiling hook. "We need to hurry."

Talon nodded, pulling down a lantern of his own before he broke into a run. His feet pounded against the stone of the corridor as his gaze searched the darkness ahead in the hope of seeing something. There was only blackness. He pushed himself harder, trying to pick up speed. He could hear Brianne and the soldier at his heels. The tunnel led upwards, a slight slope to it.

"Maybe he lied," Brianne said.

He better not have or he'd be going back to have another talk to him and this one wouldn't be as friendly. "Then we'll soon know." He'd barely spoken the words when they reached another closed door and he came to a stop. Talon tried to open it. "It's locked too.

"Out of the way." The soldier pushed past him, swinging the axe.

Talon jumped back as splinters flew around him.

"Hurry up," Brianne urged. "We don't want the messenger to get away."

With a crack, the door splintered around the lock, opening to a pale sky, the sun nearly ready to rise above the horizon. Talon shouted, "Stop," and the reddish-brown robed figure glanced over his shoulder before he tried to run faster, his robes bunched up around his thighs. Placing his lantern on the ground, Talon started to reach for his sword, tensing to run after the man.

Leaving her lantern behind, Brianne stepped up beside Talon, her arrow already pulled back in her bow. "He's not getting away." She let go of the string and the arrow travelled through the air, another one ready.

Talon's hand remained on the hilt of his sword as he stayed beside Brianne. The man stumbled as the arrow hit him in the leg. He tried to continue, glancing over his shoulder as he stumbled onwards. When Talon was about to move forward, Brianne let another arrow go. This time, when the arrow pierced his other leg, the man fell to the ground and Brianne lowered her bow.

"Let's find out what he knows." She broke into a run.

Talon sprinted after her, reaching the man as she did, the soldier several steps behind them. The man writhed on the ground, cursing, as Talon stared down at him. How had these people managed to fool them for so long?

The soldier used the head of the axe to press the man to the ground. "Are you the only one?"

The man nodded frantically. "Help me. Please help me. The arrows."

"The arrows will be a splinter compared to what we'll do if you don't answer," Brianne said.

"I'm the only one. Help me."

Talon felt no sympathy, but he also didn't feel the

satisfaction he'd expected to feel. He held out his hand. "The message."

"My legs," the man moaned. "Help me. I don't want to lose my legs."

"Give us the message." The soldier drew the axe back. "Or your legs won't be a problem. They'll be gone."

"No. No. Wait." The man rummaged in his belt pouch. "Wait. Please wait." He dropped the folded piece of paper as he drew it out.

Talon grabbed hold of the message, opening the page to see a messy scrawl. He held it out to Brianne, relieved they'd intercepted it. "It says the House and earthly dwelling have been attacked and for the garrisons to strike immediately."

Taking the message, Brianne's gaze scanned the page before she handed it to the soldier. She glanced over as two soldiers came running towards them. "Let the First Officer know. We'll get this man back into the city. We also need the doors fixed and guards to keep anyone from wandering in and out."

The soldier handed the letter onto his companions. "My thoughts exactly. You two see the First Officer. Send back the first couple of soldiers you see to guard the door. I'll help with the prisoner."

With a nod, the two soldiers ran towards the

smashed door of the corridor. From the outside it looked like a rundown shack.

Talon stared down at their prisoner who was still moaning. "How are we going to do this?"

"I vote with a knife," Brianne said.

"We're not to kill him," the soldier said.

"A pity. He's really starting to annoy me."

Talon had to agree with Brianne. A knife was exactly what the Prilonian needed to quieten his complaints and drawn out groans. "Grab a hold of one of his arms." He directed the comment to the soldier. "If he can't walk we'll drag him back." The prisoner started to shout in protest, but Talon ignored him, determined to get the man to the city.

The soldier grabbed the other arm and they hoisted him to his feet.

Brianne stood with a hand on her hip, glaring at the prisoner. "Shut up," She snapped when the man's whining got louder.

"You're going to kill me," he moaned.

"Shut up or I will," Brianne muttered.

"Not until we finish finding out what he knows," the soldier said.

Talon nodded. "Yes, things like where the new recruits go."

Chapter Thirty-Five

Brianne

At Talon's words, anger had Brianne in the prisoner's face, her dagger at his throat, her bow on the ground where she'd stood. "Where are they? What have you done to Zinervie?"

"You'll never save her."

Not the words she wanted to hear. "Tell me or you'll never have the chance to speak again."

"You won't get away with this. New Prilonia will send more troops when none of our regular messages come through."

"When's the next one due?" Talon asked.

"We need to get him back for questioning," the soldier said.

"Where is Zinervie," Brianne demanded.

The prisoner's expression of fear changed to one

of smugness. "Their wings are removed as soon as they're taken to New Prilonia. One out of every ten don't make it."

His words made her anger explode. She drew her arm back to stab him. Her wrist was caught at the same time as the prisoner's expression turned to one of fear and he dropped to the ground where he lay screaming, trying to drag himself away. The soldier grabbed Brianne's other arm and she tried to pull away from him and Talon, who was warning the soldier to let her go.

Soldiers dropped down around them, Ewyn amongst them and only Talon was left to keep her back from the prisoner, his arms around her waist as she struggled to get free.

When Ewyn ordered several soldiers to fly the prisoner back to the city, Brianne screamed, "No. Make him tell us where Zinervie is. They're going to cut off her wings." She remembered Ewyn had organised aerial searches. "Have they found her? And what about Macklyn? Did he say anything?" She stopped fighting Talon's arms and sank back against his chest.

"Meet me at your grandfather's home. We've got a lot to discuss." Ewyn turned to his soldiers, pointing to three of them. "Guard the door." He pointed to another one. "Arrange to have it fixed." Then he faced Brianne. "Get there as soon as you can." He launched into the air.

"Wait." Brianne pulled away from Talon. "What about Zinervie?"

Ewyn ignored her, flying towards the city wall.

Brianne stared after him, anger and frustration making her want to grab her bow and bring him out of the sky. He better have some answers for her when she reached her grandfather's home. Striding back to her bow, she picked it up, heading towards the busted door.

Talon fell into step beside her. "They'll get more information out of him if he's alive."

Brianne stopped, turning to face him. "Would you have let him live if he'd sent Marshall into slavery?"

"No, but I hope you'd have stopped me because later I'd be wondering what information I could have got out of him to help me find Marshall."

It took a few moments for the worst of her anger to fade, replaced by relief. "Thank you."

Talon grinned. "Any time. Just make sure you do the same for me."

Brianne returned his grin fleetingly, unable to maintain it for more than a second at the thought of Zinervie in the hands of the enemy, regretting not being a better friend. They had to find her. "I will." She glanced towards the door. "Let's find out what my uncle has to say. It better be good." The last was muttered under her breath as she strode towards the door.

It didn't take long for them to return to Briant's home and Talon flew them up to the balcony more smoothly this time. What did take long was waiting for Briant and Ewyn to return.

A noise at the front door interrupted Brianne's pacing and before she had a chance to speak, her mother ran towards her, wrapping her arms around her, kissing each of her cheeks.

Talon came to a halt at Brianne's side, taking a step back when Brianne complained, "Mum, you're crushing me."

Ailis didn't loosen her hold. "They said you were dead. I'm going to kill Ewyn. How dare he do that to me."

Brianne finally managed to pull away slightly. "Not until he tells me what I want to know, then you can." She turned so she could smile at Talon. "Talon, I want you to meet my mum, Ailis."

With an arm still around her daughter, Ailis faced Talon. "You have wings."

He nodded warily.

"Mum!"

"They told me you'd brought a Tersten back with you. They never said anything about wings. And they should have told me you were back last night. Instead they risked you in another battle and waited until this morning to tell me."

Brianne pulled away, moving to stand beside Talon. "I'm fine. It's what I've been trained for."

"You nearly died," Ailis protested.

Brianne shook her head. "Not even close." She sent a warning glance to Talon. He better not mention her dive off the wall. Smiling for her mother's benefit, she said, "See, unharmed and ready for the next mission."

Ewyn entered the room. "Good, because we've got something you and Talon can help us with."

"I won't go against my people," Talon said.

"We want to join your people. We tried previously, but the squad we sent out under a flag of truce was slaughtered," Ewyn said.

Briant entered the room, glancing around at everyone in his living room. "What is everyone doing standing around here? My office, now." When Ailis started to move, he pointed at her. "Not you, Ailis. Army matters aren't your concern anymore."

"If it's about my daughter, it is my concern."

"Mum." Brianne's tone was filled with exasperation and annoyance at being treated like a child.

When Ewyn started to argue with Ailis, Brianne shook her head, grabbed Talon's hand and pulled him from the room. Once they were alone in the office, she let his hand go. "Thank you."

"For what?"

"Trying to protect me from my mum."

Talon shrugged. "I didn't know who she was when she ran at you like that."

"I think in some ways she's glad I don't have wings because it should have kept me out of the army."

Briant entered the office before Talon could say anything. He pointed to the stools in front of his desk. "Sit down." He seated himself behind the desk, not waiting for them to sit before he continued speaking. "We need to know if the Terstens will fight with us. If not, will they let us cross their lands to attack the garrisons."

Talon remained standing. "I don't know. Marshall and Garnet are trying to find people willing to help, but I don't know what has happened while we've been here."

"They were pretty certain they'd find help." Brianne sat down, leaning forward. "When do we leave? And what about Zinervie?"

"Slow down. No one is going anywhere for about a week. We're putting the entire country into lockdown so we can capture every Prilonian. We'll tell the civilians there has been an unusually large amount of Tersten squads sighted. The order has gone out that anyone travelling during the lockdown will be taken captive. That means we should be able to find Zinervie and the other two more easily."

Relief washed through Brianne as she nodded her agreement.

"Not squads, units," Talon corrected. "What are we meant to do while we're waiting?"

Brianne grinned at him. "How about learning to fly?"

"I can fly." Talon looked offended.

Brianne nodded slowly, her grin still in place. "You keep telling yourself that."

"I'll teach you," Briant said.

"What?" Brianne stared at her grandfather. He'd long since passed the stage where he needed to train fledglings.

"You heard me."

"Why?"

"Because I'm not having some fledgling flying you around and getting you killed."

"I can fly," Talon protested.

Brianne ignored him, continuing to talk to her grandfather. "When can you start?"

Chapter Thirty-Six

Talon

Talon watched as Brianne's mother held onto her. A stab of envy hit him when Brianne tried to pull away and her mother's arms tightened around her. Still holding Brianne tight, Ailis kissed Brianne's cheeks. Spending nearly a week with Brianne's family had shown him how little he and his sister had meant to their parents. Terst was their priority. All else was far less important to them, including their children.

Brianne finally managed to pull away from her mother. "I'll be fine."

"Be careful," Ailis said.

Before Brianne could answer, Briant stepped forward, placing a hand on his daughter's shoulder. "Let her go, Ailis. She's more than capable of completing this mission successfully."

Talon watched as Brianne walked over to Conal, the soldier who'd broken down the tunnel doors, and turned so he could carry her. Briant had ordered Talon not to fly Brianne unless it was an emergency. Not until he learned how to fly properly. It was probably a good thing Briant hadn't seen his first attempts at flying.

He launched himself into the air flying with the squad to the border town where they'd arranged to have horses waiting for him and Brianne. As much as he hated to leave the Tersten horses behind, flying covered the ground a lot faster. If it hadn't been for the Prilonians' interference, the Caelians probably would have killed his people off with how quickly they could cross the land. But, if it hadn't been for the Prilonians' interference their people would never have been enemies.

When they reached the town, Talon was glad to land, his wings were aching. But not in the way they once had, more in the way of muscles that are not accustomed to a new task. Several soldiers came to meet them, leading him, Brianne and Conal to an office.

Conal saluted the man seated behind the desk. "Third Officer."

"Take a seat." The Third Officer gestured his aide over. "Fetch another stool."

"I'll stand," Talon said.

The Third Officer nodded, waving his aide away. He slid two letters across his desk towards Conal. "We thought these might help you take the Holy City. They talk about two hidden exits, focusing on one that's damaged and needs repairs. The details in the letter should be enough for your soldiers to find the damaged one."

"Holy City?" Talon asked.

Brianne nodded. "Don't you have one?"

"No."

"Where does Elden go when he supposedly does his communing with the gods?"

Talon shrugged. "I have no idea. Probably to your land by the sounds of it."

Brianne stared at him for a moment. "Of course he does. I didn't think about that. Then why does he need the Holy City?"

"Probably somewhere to go when he needs a break from destroying our people." Conal slid the letters into his belt pouch. "I'll give these to the First Officer when I return. Was there anything else, sir?"

The Third Officer shook his head. "No, that's all.

Do you need more than the two horses and saddlebags of gear we readied?"

"No, sir. Thank you for this," Brianne said.

The Third Officer rose to his feet, coming around the desk. "I'm the one who should thank you. My son had planned to join the House on his next birthday." He held out his hand to Brianne. When she had shaken it, he turned to Talon and did the same. "If you need anything, anything at all, let me know."

When they were outside, waiting for the horses to be brought to them, Talon said to Brianne. "I thought you said friends exchange kisses on the cheeks. I've only ever seen your mother do that." His attention was momentarily caught by Conal, taking to the air with his squad and flying in the direction they'd come from.

Brianne grinned. "Only family." She paused. "And very close friends." She strode towards the boy who led two horses towards them.

Talon stared after her for a moment, then grinned as he strode towards her. Mounting his horse, he rode beside Brianne, waiting until they were out of the town before he spoke. "How close a friend?"

Brianne laughed. "I was still feeling grateful you'd survived your so called flying, not to mention I was about to enter the House and didn't know if I was going to get out alive."

She couldn't have been that grateful if all she'd managed was a couple of kisses on his cheeks. "Next time I'll show you how we show we're glad someone is still alive," Talon said.

Brianne laughed again. "I hope it's better than your flying."

"Stop picking on my flying." He started to say it was better than hers, then he recalled how she'd reacted when they were practising and he'd said he'd clip her wings so she couldn't fly around the room. No, he wouldn't say those words to her.

They remained quiet as they crossed the land, the country changing from dry red dust and rock pillars with the odd area of brown grass and stunted trees to yellowed meadows with taller trees. By late afternoon, the country had become lush meadows and shady trees with the Feronian Mountains visible in the distance.

After how quickly they'd crossed the country earlier by wings, horseback seemed unbearably slow. No wonder Brianne envied him his wings. Since he'd stopped hiding them, he was actually finding them useful.

As they approached the cave, they slowed. Talon

looked around. Everything was quiet. He dismounted and tied his horse to a tree. When Brianne started to dismount, he shook his head. "Wait here. I'll see if it's safe. No point both of us walking into danger." He drew his sword as he walked towards the cave entrance, his gaze travelling around the area, his steps soft.

Nothing moved and there were no unusual sounds. He slipped inside the cave, his eyes straining to see in the darkness. The sound of a sword being drawn from a scabbard had him stepping to the side, hiding in the shadows. "Who's there?"

"Telling you isn't going to make you want to sheath your sword."

"Bellamy." The word was a curse. "Where's my sister?"

"Her and Merel have gone to get water."

"Who?"

"Some annoying friend of Garnet's who thinks I'm the love of her life."

"Has she suffered a head injury?" Talon inched his way around the edge of the cave.

"Probably," Bellamy said dryly. "I can hear you moving. Do you think I'm about to stand still and let you kill me?"

Talon looked in the direction Bellamy's voice now came from. "Why are you here?"

"Because it's my turn to guard the cave."

"And you're doing that in the dark?" He wished Bellamy would stand still.

"I barely had time to get the fire out when I heard you outside. Couldn't you have called out to let me know it was you? Do you know how annoying it is to clean the dirt out of the pit before it can be relit?"

Talon bit back a curse as Bellamy's voice came from a different direction. "And let you know I was here so you could attack me while I was a target?" He waited until he finished talking before he headed for Bellamy's new location.

"Things have changed while you've been away, Talon."

The voice was in front of him and he felt the air shift as Bellamy started to move away. He reached out, grabbing hold of Bellamy, pressing his sword against Bellamy's neck. It took a great deal of effort not to kill him. His sister better be safe. "Explain quickly."

Chapter Thirty-Seven

Brianne

Brianne looked in every direction, still seated on the horse. Her bow was out in case Talon called for help. What was taking him so long? Should she check on him? The crack of a twig had her turning in that direction, her bow up and ready.

Garnet and a dark haired girl came out of the trees, freezing at the sight of her. Garnet grinned, putting her pail of water on the ground before she ran to Brianne. The other girl remained frozen.

"You were gone forever."

Brianne slid off her horse, putting her bow aside in time to catch the girl who threw herself at her. "It was only eight days." At times it had felt so much longer.

Garnet pulled back to look around. "Where's Talon?"

"In the cave." At Garnet's horrified expression, she grabbed hold of the girl's shoulders. "What? What's wrong?"

"Bellamy's in there."

Brianne ran for the cave, drawing her dagger as she did. "Talon!"

"No. It's safe." Garnet ran after her. "He's on our side. Everything's changed."

Then why hadn't Talon come out yet? "Talon?" She paused at the entrance.

"I told you to wait." There was anger in his voice.

"Garnet's out here with another girl." Brianne walked into the cave, trying to see in the darkness.

"Talon?" Garnet entered the cave.

"Garnet, tell him to let me go," Bellamy called out. "He's got a sword at my throat."

"Talon, he's on our side," Garnet said. "What happened to the fire?"

"I put it out," Bellamy said.

At the same time, Talon said, "I don't trust him. Look what he did to Warner."

"Are you still going on about that? It wasn't me, it was someone-" Bellamy's words ended abruptly.

"Don't kill him," an unfamiliar voice said from behind Brianne.

"Who are you?" Brianne demanded, shifting so her back wasn't to the girl.

"Merel." There was a waver in her voice.

"Brianne, light the fire," Talon said.

"I can't even find it." Brianne shuffled further into the cave.

"I know where it is." Garnet brushed past Brianne.

"What's been happening while we were gone," Brianne asked.

"Only the capital-" Bellamy's words ended abruptly again. After a moment he growled. "Stop that."

"Then stop talking," Talon said. "You tell me, Garnet."

"We told some people, who told other people and eventually, there was a heap of fighting." Garnet stopped and blew on the small flame that flickered to life. "It was awful. They killed a lot of Holy Ones."

"They were all impostors," Talon said.

"I know, but it's still hard to believe. Anyway, the Supreme One-"

Talon interrupted Garnet. "Elden."

Garnet shrugged in the light of the fire she was steadily feeding. "Elden took the capital. Our parents are still in there along with a lot of other people. Some escaped. The Prilonians tried sending out messengers, but we've caught every one of them. There were also some pigeons, but we shot them out of the sky."

"Who's in charge?" Brianne asked.

"A group of officers. Most of the army escaped from the capital and they're all camped in the foothills of the mountains. They plan to capture the garrisons and guard the mountain passes," Garnet said.

"We need to see them." Talon continued to hold his sword at Bellamy's throat.

"I can take you to-" Bellamy's words ended in a growl.

"Let him go, Talon," Garnet said. "He's helping us."

"Why?" Talon demanded.

"Because-" Again Bellamy's words ended abruptly.

"I didn't ask you," Talon growled.

Brianne could hear the anger in both Bellamy and Talon's voices. She moved forward, her gaze on Talon. "Remember that favour I owed you?"

"What favour?"

"The prisoner." She reached out, grasping his wrist and pulling his sword away from Bellamy.

Bellamy moved quickly, reaching Garnet's side. Merel continued to stand just inside the cave, her eyes wide, her hands pressed against her mouth.

Talon glared at Brianne, taking a step towards her,

not bothering to pull out of her grip. "It wasn't the same."

"I know. I had a reason to kill the prisoner."

"You saying I have no reason to keep Bellamy prisoner?"

She shrugged. "What do you think?" She watched as his gaze brushed past her. Then it hit her, she had her back to a possible enemy and it didn't bother her at all because Talon could see him.

"What's wrong?" Talon's tone was urgent.

Brianne shook her head, letting go of him and stepping to the side. When had she learned to completely trust him? Trust him so thoroughly she took it for granted he'd watch her back. "Nothing. We need to see whoever's in charge." She turned towards Bellamy. "Why are you here?" When Talon started to speak, she elbowed him in the ribs.

"Because I won't work for the enemy. And anyone who has enslaved our people is the enemy."

Brianne gave him a short, sharp nod. They were words she could understand. "We need to speak to whoever's in charge. My people want to discuss a combined attack on the garrisons."

"As soon as we put out the fire we can go," Bellamy said. "We were only waiting around here for you to turn up."

"But I just relit it," Garnet protested.

"Put it out," Talon ordered. "And where's Marshall?"

"Patrolling with his unit," Garnet said.

"He should be looking after you."

Garnet stopped tipping dirt over the fire from a pail that was beside it. "I can look after myself."

"We've been taking turns waiting here with her," Bellamy said.

Talon ignored him. "He said he'd look after you."

Brianne glanced towards the opening of the cave. Daylight was struggling to enter. "I'd like to get to where we're going before it's dark, if possible."

"It's less than an hour away." Bellamy gathered his gear.

She bit back a sigh. What she wouldn't give for wings right now. She was sick of being stuck on the back of a horse. It wasn't natural. Her people were made for soaring through the sky.

Chapter Thirty-Eight

Talon

Talon stood at the edge of the campsite, staring into the star-studded night. His father had probably been right about him not making a good general. He'd had to walk away from the bickering. Some had wanted to ally themselves with the Caelians while many still didn't trust them. Brianne had pointed out they'd once been allies until the Prilonians had tricked them. He'd left her there, arguing. They'd probably waste the rest of the night and still not make a decision.

Hearing footsteps headed his way he turned and saw Brianne. Lantern light showed how tired she looked. She was stopped by Bellamy. It took all his willpower not to march over and tell Bellamy to leave her alone. His hands tightened into fists as she smiled at Bellamy, nodding her head before she continued walking towards him, stepping out of the light from the lantern that had been hung nearby.

"What did he want?" Talon demanded when Brianne reached his side, nodding towards Bellamy.

"To tell me it wasn't him who did wrong by Warner, but someone trying to make trouble for him."

"Who?"

"He doesn't know, but he did say he knew it wasn't you."

"Really?" He didn't even bother keeping the derision from his voice.

"Yes. He said if you wanted to get even with him you wouldn't go behind his back to do it."

"Maybe he's not a complete idiot, but I still don't trust him."

"I wasn't asking you to."

They fell silent a while, both staring out into the night until Talon broke the silence. "Have they stopped arguing yet?" He wanted to get on with planning the attack, not listen to them decide who to trust. They shouldn't trust anyone.

"No. Bellamy was on his way to see what they were up to."

"Do you have to bring him into every conversation?" Talon growled. His sister had done it on the ride to the encampment. Anyone would think he was one of the gods come to visit.

"What's so terrible about him?"

Talon started to point out Bellamy's faults, then decided to try a different tactic. "What was so terrible about Macklyn?"

"He told everyone I was dead."

"You hated him before then."

Brianne took ages to reply. "He always had to be better than me."

Talon nodded. "Exactly."

They fell silent again. The next break in the silence was when a noise drew Talon's attention and he swore.

"What?" Brianne turned to face the direction of his gaze.

"Bellamy," Talon muttered. He was the last person he wanted to see, but it looked like Bellamy planned to join them regardless of how welcome he was.

Bellamy came to a stop in front of them. "They've finished arguing."

"What did they decide?" Brianne asked.

Talon was glad it was Brianne who asked, he'd rather not have to talk to him.

"They've agreed to help, on their terms," Bellamy said.

"What are their terms?" Brianne asked.

"I don't know, they wouldn't tell me, only sent me to get you."

Talon walked beside Brianne, dreading putting up with more bickering. He was certain they weren't going to like the terms. When he stepped inside, he soon found he was wrong.

Brianne held up a hand, interrupting one of the officers who started to speak. "There's no point discussing terms with me, I don't have the authority. I've been asked to set up a meeting. If you have a map I can show you the three sites they've offered as possible meeting places. They're on the border and open enough so you can see there's no risk of ambush."

Talon shook his head, disgusted by the fresh wave of arguments Brianne's words brought. By the time a meeting place was decided upon and they were shown to a tent, Brianne was yawning.

"They're so lucky I didn't have my bow with me," Brianne muttered as she lay atop the bedroll set out on one side of the tent, a lantern sitting on the ground at her head. She hadn't been allowed to take the bow into the meeting. It was waiting in the tent for her.

Talon tugged off his boots once he sat on the other

bedroll. "I hope they don't expect us to be at the meeting or I'm likely to hand you your bow."

Brianne chuckled sleepily. "Put your boots back on." She closed her eyes, still on top of the bedroll.

"Why?"

"We're at war. Do you want to fight barefoot if we're attacked in the night?"

Talon stared at her, lying within arm's reach. His gaze travelled over curves before returning to her face.

Brianne opened a single eye. "Go to sleep." She closed her eye again.

Talon leaned forward. "Open your eyes."

She kept them closed. "Why?"

"Open them." Several minutes passed before she opened her eyes. He stared at clear blue eyes. "They've changed colour."

"You woke me to tell me that?"

Talon slowly smiled. "You weren't asleep."

"Just about," she grumbled. "So you kept me awake to tell me my eyes have changed colour."

"No. I kept you awake so I could see what they looked like."

"Go to sleep, Talon." She rolled to face the side of the tent.

He leant forward so he could see her face clearly.

Her eyes were closed. "I like them." Moving away, he sat on his bedroll and started to pull his boots back on.

Brianne rolled to face him, her eyes open, a slight smile on her lips. "Were you expecting a compliment in return?"

Talon grinned. "I thought you were going to sleep."

"I'm trying to, but someone won't shut up and put the light out."

Talon finished pulling on his boots and reached for the lantern, turning it off. "Goodnight, Brianne." He lay on his stomach, letting his wings out. He felt a hand brush across his feathers.

"This is what I like. Much better than ordinary blue eyes."

He captured her hand, linking his fingers through hers. "What happened to the feather of mine you took?"

"It's in my belt pouch."

He tried to see her in the darkness, wishing he hadn't put the lantern out.

"Goodnight, Talon." Her voice was soft and drowsy.

He momentarily tightened his fingers on hers before he closed his own eyes and tried to sleep.

Morning would come too soon and they had to ride for the border and finish arranging the meeting.

Chapter Thirty-Nine

Brianne

The next morning Brianne glared at Talon, wishing she had something to hit him with. "Shut up and let's get going. It'll take long enough to get to the border without you slowing things down."

"He's not coming with us." Talon sent a glare in Bellamy's direction.

"We don't have a choice. Your people didn't ask, they ordered us to take him. Of course they're going to choose Bellamy. They know you hate him. Besides, he's not that bad." She regretted the last few words the moment she spoke them and saw Talon's expression.

"We don't need him. He'll slow us down."

She reached for Talon's hand, but he pulled away from her. "Talon-"

"I don't trust him."

Again she tried to take hold of his hand, stepping close to him. This time he let her. "I know we don't need him. Even I'll slow you down. Having Bellamy with us means you can fly ahead to let my people know and I'll have backup in case I need it."

"You'd trust him to fight at your back?" Talon pulled his hand from her grasp.

Brianne nearly growled. She couldn't say anything right this morning. Losing patience she jabbed at his chest with a finger. "Quit whining and get on your horse. We don't have a choice. He's coming with us. Get over it." She strode towards her horse that was tied to a hitching post near where Bellamy stood with his own horse. Mounting, she shot another glare at Talon, who continued to stand where she'd left him, then headed in the direction of the border.

Bellamy joined her and within minutes Talon brought his horse along the opposite side to Bellamy. Most of the journey to the border was made in silence. A few times Bellamy started a conversation, but most of them were abruptly ended by Talon.

When they drew closer to the border, Brianne asked Talon to fly ahead. It took an argument to convince him. She watched him fly off, leading his horse from her own. "What happened between you two?"

"I stole his girlfriend when we were sixteen."

"Why?"

Bellamy shrugged. "I don't remember all the details now. We were always in competition with each other. There was some stupid argument and he said something about having a girlfriend and that no one was even slightly interested in being with me." He grinned. "What else could I do with a challenge like that?"

Brianne slowly shook her head. "Ignore it?"

Bellamy laughed. "Sure." A moment passed before he continued. "She wasn't worth fighting over. A week later she ditched me for someone else. He wouldn't have had her long even without me interfering. She was always looking for someone better."

They fell into silence as they continued to ride towards the border. It wasn't long before two squads flew towards them, a dark winged figure amongst them. Brianne halted her horse, and dismounted. The small amount of ground she could cover before they reached her wasn't worth worrying about.

"They're friends?" Bellamy dismounted, his hand dropping to the hilt of the sword he wore at his side.

"You could say that."

"What would you say?"

"That's my grandfather on Talon's right and my uncle on his left. You might want to almost close your eyes as they come closer or they'll be full of dust when they land."

Bellamy nodded, but his hand stayed on the hilt of his sword.

Briant was the first to land, reaching out a hand to rest it on Brianne's shoulder. "I knew you could manage, Sprite."

With a sharp nod, she gestured towards Bellamy. "Grandad, this is Bellamy. Bellamy, Officer Finnin."

Bellamy held out his hand with a respectful nod. "Sir."

Briant shook the hand before he turned back to Brianne. "You happy with the plan for us to meet so far into their territory?"

"Yes. It made sense. Now we don't have to wait for them to reach the border before we start making plans to attack."

"Are they to be trusted?" Ewyn asked.

Brianne grinned. "Is anyone?"

Ewyn answered her with a grin of his own before he turned to a soldier behind him. "Take the map the Tersten showed us and get everyone moving. We'll go on ahead." He turned to another soldier. "You bring their horses to the meeting point."

"How are we to get there?" Bellamy asked.

"Hope you're not afraid of heights." Ewyn called forward another one of his soldiers. "You take the dirt walker. Conal, you take my niece."

They travelled back much quicker, reaching the meeting place well before the appointed time. The Terstens were setting up tents to use as meeting rooms.

Once introductions were made, Briant took Brianne aside. "Go see Conal. Take your boy with you." He gestured towards Talon with his head.

"Why?"

"Off with you. You'll find out soon enough. I have other matters to deal with."

Brianne watched her grandfather. He strode back to the cluster of officers chatting while they waited for their meeting space to be prepared so they could get down to serious business. She noticed that someone had listened to her and had provided stools for her people to sit on. They must have raided every farmhouse in the area to get enough chairs and stools for everyone, if the mismatched furniture was anything to go by.

It didn't take Brianne long to collect Talon and

find Conal. What did take time was finding somewhere private to speak. She glared at Bellamy who had followed them.

"I have my orders," Bellamy said.

"This doesn't concern you," Brianne said.

"If we flew away he wouldn't be able to follow," Talon said.

"It'd end the meeting. They're worried you two are planning something so the Caelians end up winning," Bellamy said.

Brianne sighed. "Why does everyone have to complicate things?" She turned to Conal. "Should we wait or can he hear what you've got to say?"

Conal stared at her a moment before he answered. "They want the two of you to try and find the rebels."

Brianne was certain she must have misheard. "Cross the Feronian Mountains?"

Conal nodded. "They think a small party would have a better chance of sneaking in."

"Why do they want the rebels found?" Talon asked.

"To keep the Prilonians busy on all sides, especially when we take the Holy City," Conal said.

"They still haven't captured it?"

Conal shook his head. "No, but no one can get out. Both the tunnels have been found and we've stopped several escape attempts. It was decided the garrisons should be the first priority. We don't want the Prilonians coming over those mountains unexpectedly."

"I'm going with you," Bellamy stated.

"No." Talon's hand rested on the hilt of his sword, his wings still out.

Brianne placed a hand on Talon's arm in the hope it would stop him from drawing his sword. "He won't be able to go where we're going. We'll have to fly to reach the top of the mountain if we want to avoid being caught."

Talon grinned. "I guess the dirt walker will have to stay behind."

She nearly laughed at how he managed to put the right amount of derision in the term, but thought that wouldn't be a good idea. She spoke to Bellamy. "You can come to the foot of the mountains and wait for us to return if you want."

"No. You can't expect my people to let yours make all the decisions," Bellamy said.

"The Terstens are my people too." Talon took a step towards Bellamy.

"Not since you grew wings. No one trusts you not to side with the birds." Bellamy put the same amount of derision in the word birds as Talon had put in dirt walker.

"I'll take him."

Brianne turned to Conal. "What?"

"The dirt walker. I'll take him up the mountain." He grinned. "And I'll even promise not to let go of him when we're in the sky."

Bellamy took a step back, eyeing Conal. He was silent a moment before he nodded. "I'll let my superiors know." He started to walk away then turned back to face them. "If you leave without me, it'll end the negotiations."

Brianne watched him stride away. This was going to be interesting. She wasn't sure how she was going to keep Talon and Bellamy from killing each other.

"I'll let the First Officer know." Conal strode away when Brianne nodded.

Talon stared after the two retreating figures. "We could leave now."

"No, you heard him. We can't risk ending the meeting."

"I don't trust him."

Brianne met his gaze. "Do you trust me?"

Talon nodded without hesitation. "Yes."

"Then we'll watch each other's backs. We'll be fine."

Talon nodded slowly. "I'll make sure of it."

Chapter Forty

Talon

Talon wrapped his arms around Brianne's chest, pulling her against him as he gripped her shoulders, her bow in her hand. They'd spent the night camped in the foothills, not wanting to cross the mountains in the dark. A faint hint of light filled the air as he and Conal, carrying Bellamy who held a crossbow, flew into the sky. Talon didn't like having to leave his own crossbow slung low on his back between his wings when Bellamy was armed. It felt wrong. Conal pulled ahead and he wanted to race him. Instead he controlled the urge to win knowing he'd never reach the summit if he didn't pace himself.

Brianne tilted her head towards him. "I love the feel of this. Flying is the best sensation in the world."

It was easy for her to say. She didn't have to force

her way through the air. Didn't have to make uncooperative wings tilt at the right angle to go in the correct direction. And didn't have to worry about landing when she reached her destination. He was over halfway up the mountain when it became a struggle to keep heading skywards. The summit didn't look any closer and muscles, that he hadn't known existed, ached. Conal continued to head for the summit and Talon forced himself on.

Once Conal was over the top of the mountain, Talon couldn't see him. Was he expected to fly down the other side? That wasn't going to happen. Trees brushed against his feet as he crested the summit, barely able to maintain his height. Spotting Conal and Bellamy in a clearing on the upper slopes of the mountain, Talon forced his wings to tilt so he could reach his destination before he crashed. Bellamy would never tire of telling everyone if that happened.

Talon staggered as he landed, barely keeping his feet, his arms tightening on Brianne. When he loosened his grip, she turned to him with a grin.

"We made it." Brianne slung her bow on her back.

Talon nodded then grinned. "You sound surprised you're still alive."

"Well, considering your flying skill I probably should be."

"Then I guess it's time to teach you how my people show we're glad someone is still alive." He tugged her to him, his lips meeting hers. Their lips had barely touched, when the sound of a sword being drawn caused him to jump backwards and draw his own.

Conal stood in front of him, his axe held ready. "Keep your hands off her."

Bellamy stood between Talon and Conal, his sword drawn. "Put your axe away."

"Everyone put their weapons away," Brianne ordered.

Talon looked from Conal to Bellamy, surprised Bellamy had come to his defence. He took another step back and lowered his sword.

"All of you." Brianne looked from one to the other. "Hurry up."

Conal and Bellamy lowered their weapons.

"He had no right to do that," Conal said. "Your grandfather told me to watch out for you."

"If I had wanted him to stop, I'd have held a dagger at his throat. I don't need you to interfere," Brianne said. "Now put your weapons away." When none of them moved, she threw her hands up in the air. "Fine. I'll find the rebels on my own." She strode towards the edge of the clearing.

Talon hurried after her, his sword still drawn. "You can't go off on your own."

Brianne turned, opening her mouth, but her words were left unsaid as she looked to the side of Talon.

Talon turned to see what had caught her attention. Flying across the top of the Feronian Mountains, towards them, were three winged men. One with white wings, one with a mixture of white and brown and one with a mixture of black and brown feathers. Talon's sword came up again and he noticed Conal and Bellamy also raising their weapons.

Brianne drew her own sword, stepping up to Talon's side. "Looks like the rebels might have found us."

"Doesn't mean they're going to be happy they've found us," Talon said.

The three men came closer, bows out, arrows aimed at them. The man with the black and brown feathers called out, "Drop your weapons."

Talon fought the urge to step in front of Brianne. It would be a pointless effort, only annoy her and she'd step out from behind him anyway. "If we do that, you'll probably kill us." Talon kept his sword raised.

"Drop your weapons and we'll let you live long enough to explain what you're doing here," the rebel said.

"We're attacking the Prilonians," Brianne said.

All three rebels laughed. The white winged one said, "Four against an entire nation. Likely story."

"By nightfall all the garrisons will have fallen," Bellamy said.

"I think they're serious," the white winged one said to his companions.

"We know who they are now. They can't manipulate us anymore," Brianne said.

"How could you not have known who they were?" the black and brown feathers demanded.

Talon lowered his sword and took a step towards them. "Put away your weapons and we'll tell you everything, including all about the army headed this way." He watched as they held a whispered conversation, before finally lowering their weapons.

Black and brown feathers spoke. "I'm Lyle Paget, that's Sorrell Thayer." He pointed to the man with the white and brown feathers. "And that's Torrey Patton." This time he pointed to the man with white feathers.

"I'm Talon Morin, this is Brianne Devin, Bellamy Allard and Conal." He pointed to each in turn, but didn't know Conal's last name to be able to give it.

"Conal Haden," Conal said.

Lyle dropped to the ground, folding his wings so

they cloaked his back. "My mother was a Morin. An old army family."

"My family have always served in the army." Talon didn't bother mentioning his father was the current general. He was no longer proud of that fact.

Bellamy sheathed his sword. "How wonderful. Looks like you found a long lost cousin." Sarcasm laced his tone. "Now the family reunion is over, think we can get to the reason we were dragged up here."

"No one invited you," Talon said.

"No, but I was ordered to join you."

Brianne stepped between them, sheathing her sword. "If you children could leave your bickering till later, we need to figure out how to take back our country."

"Iralen is our country," Sorrell said.

"It doesn't look that way. I'd say it's currently the Prilonian's country," Bellamy pointed out. "Don't they call it New Prilonia?"

Conal pointed a finger at Bellamy. "If you keep making comments like that dirt walker, I will be dropping you off the nearest cliff."

"Need help finding one?" Talon asked.

"Why would your people send an argumentative bunch like you lot?" Lyle asked.

"I guess we just got lucky," Talon said dryly.

Lyle shook his head. "Not what I'd call it. Come on, we'll take you to our camp so we can talk. It's only a short flight." His wings snapped out.

Talon wanted to protest, but he wasn't a dirt walker. He stretched his own wings, sheathing his sword as he faced Brianne. He waited for her to turn her back to him, once she'd removed her bow.

Chapter Forty-One

Brianne finished off the last of the sweet bread they'd been given, licking her fingers clean. She sat beside Lyle who was telling her about the fight against the Prilonians. Talon sat across from them, on the other side of a small campfire, and glared at Lyle. Conal talked with the other two rebels while Bellamy leaned against a tree by himself, not far from two tents half hidden amongst the trees.

When there was a pause in Lyle's conversation, Brianne interrupted with the question she'd wanted to ask for a while. "Why have you got brown feathers?"

"Prilonian ancestry. My grandmother was an escaped slave. She was pregnant with my father when she got away."

Brianne thought of Zinervie. "Do many slaves escape?"

"Some, and we help as many as possible to escape," Lyle said.

"How long after they bring them here do they remove their wings?"

"That's done before they bring them over the mountains."

Brianne stared at Lyle. "Are you sure?"

He nodded. "I've been on patrol at the summit for a couple of years now. I've never seen them brought over with their wings intact. Seen them brought over bandaged and half dead though."

"Then where do they do it?"

"I don't know. It's almost impossible to rescue first generation slaves to ask them. They keep a better eye on them since they're more likely to escape than ones born to slavery. None of us have ever made it down the other side of the mountains. Too many patrols to avoid on foot and too many archers shooting us out of the sky if we fly down. I'm surprised you made it up here."

Brianne wondered if that was because there were no Terstens to shoot what they thought were Caelians out of the sky. "And you're certain my people are never brought over with wings."

"Positive."

"Then where-" she broke off in mid sentence. The Holy City. There was none in Terst and the only difference between Terstens and Caelians were wings. That had to be where they did it. There was nowhere else. "I think I know where they do it. The Holy City."

"I can't believe they managed to trick all of you for so long. Surely someone should have realised your Holy Ones were fake," Lyle said.

"I can't believe you have Holy Ones." Brianne thought of the robes worn by the Holy Ones in Caelis and Terst. "Do yours cover themselves completely?"

"Yes, of course. How else can they give their identity to the gods? We also have to keep our Holy Ones well hidden because the Prilonians kill them on sight. They have their own gods and find ours offensive."

Sorrell joined them. "We should be on patrol, keeping an eye out for Prilonian soldiers."

"Today we should get close to one of the garrisons. I want to be there to see one taken down. It's been a long time coming." Lyle rose to his feet and held out a hand to help Brianne to hers.

She let him help her up, dusting her trousers off once she stood. "Will you help attack the garrison?"

"No, we wouldn't want to be mistaken for the enemy," Lyle said.

"Do Prilonians have wings?" Brianne asked.

"They think wings are unnatural," Sorrell said. "They believe we're abominations."

Brianne thought of Elden preaching about wingless abominations. Maybe all Caelians were abominations in his eyes. "If Prilonians don't have wings, how can you be mistaken for them? Besides, they'll know us. We can let them know you're on our side," Brianne said.

"That hasn't been decided yet." Lyle's wings snapped out. "You want a lift?"

Brianne shook her head, looking towards Talon who had joined them. "No." She smiled at him. "I'll take my chances with Talon." She took her bow from where it hung at her back and crossed the few steps between them.

"Take your chances?" Talon asked.

Brianne nearly laughed at Talon's expression. Instead she turned away from him so he could wrap his arms around her.

When Talon landed after a short flight, nearly crashing into a tree, she began to wonder if she should have taken Lyle up on his offer. She instantly discarded that thought. There was no way she would have been able to bring herself to trust Lyle not to drop her. She didn't know him that well.

She strode towards where Lyle had landed, her bow still in hand. "Where's the garrison."

"Not far. We go on foot from here so they can't see us as easily." Lyle began to walk. "They have weapons that cut through wings. They don't kill, it's the fall that does that."

"We're attacking first on foot and then by air," Brianne said.

"That should work. How did you come up with that plan?" Sorrel asked.

Talon walked at her left. "From the information we gained from reading the correspondence of the House."

"Quiet now," Lyle said. "We're getting close."

They reached the end of the forested area, a large expanse of cleared land around a small, fortified two-storey tower in front of them. Atop were men with what looked like an overgrown crossbow.

Lyle moved close to Brianne. "Where's your army?"

Brianne first searched the trees then skyward. "They shouldn't be too far away."

Talon came close to her other side. "We should take out the soldiers on top of the garrison."

Lyle shook his head. "There are more soldiers inside. They'll be outside the moment we attack."

"Then we wait until we see our army," Talon said.

The rebels' bows were in their hands in seconds, arrows trained on them. Brianne brought up her own bow, aiming it at Lyle.

Talon and Bellamy drew their swords, Conal his axe. Brianne nearly sighed. Someone was going to get killed at this rate and she hoped it wasn't one of them. A pity since the rebels were fairly likeable when they weren't pointing weapons at them.

"What now?" Brianne demanded.

"We didn't agree to fight. You aren't going to involve us in a losing battle. We don't waste soldiers in useless attacks," Lyle said.

"It won't be a useless attack. We'll have at least a hundred soldiers attacking each garrison," Brianne said.

"If your army is so big, why did you let the Prilonians enslave you for so long," Sorrell asked.

"We weren't enslaved," Talon said. "We were tricked."

"Not very bright, are you?" Torrey muttered.

Bellamy's sword pointed towards Torrey. "We

were cut off from our country and had no idea what had happened back here. Our people could only go on what the Elders told them. It isn't our fault that the ones we left behind couldn't protect a fortified city."

"They got into our defensive towers and used them against us. It was a slaughter. Taeranelle fell in hours," Torrey said.

"Guess your ancestors weren't too bright," Talon said.

"Enough." Brianne's tone was sharp. "Why are we fighting each other?" She nodded in the direction of the garrison. "The enemy is over there."

"If you're afraid to die, go hide somewhere else," Conal said. "We fight when our people arrive."

"You're insane." Lyle lowered his bow. "You know where our camp is when you're running for your lives. Just don't lead the Prilonians there. Lose them first." He gestured to his companions and they strode away through the trees.

Talon shook his head. "And they're the people we're hoping will help us? No wonder they haven't managed to beat the Prilonians in centuries. Our ancestors must have taken all the warriors with them."

"They're coming," Bellamy said.

"What?" Brianne turned to see what he meant. She saw soldiers fly above the trees, carrying foot soldiers, before they dropped out of sight. There was a shout from the garrison.

"Fan out." Conal took his bow from his back, taking an arrow from the quiver. "Time to attack."

Brianne moved away, keeping Talon in sight. When there was several feet between them, she aimed at the soldiers on top of the garrison. "Ready." Her word was echoed by Talon and Bellamy, who held crossbows.

Conal called out, "Fire."

Brianne let loose her arrow, readying a second one. Noise erupted. Soldiers poured from the garrison as Terstens came out of the forest. Brianne and her companions continued to fire at the soldiers on top of the garrison. Then the air above the garrison was filled with Caelians. A noise behind her had her turning with her bow drawn.

"Don't shoot," Lyle said.

"Why are you here?" Talon's crossbow was also trained on the three rebels.

Lyle grinned. "Seemed like a good day to die."

Talon laughed. "Then what are you waiting for? Let's take some Prilonians with us." He spun, stepped from the trees and his wings snapped out.

Brianne wanted to call him back as he launched into the air, headed for the top of the garrison. Then she immediately wished she was flying with him. The rebels followed Talon, their bows raining arrows on the Prilonians. Brianne aimed for the soldier who stepped up to the weapon on top of the garrison, taking him out before he could kill any of her people.

Time became meaningless as she fired arrow after arrow at the Prilonians around the base of the garrison. She was down to her last few, an arrow ready, when she realised there were no more targets.

Chapter Forty-Two

Talon

Talon fought inside the garrison, making his way down the stairs, his sword slashing at the remaining Prilonians, the rebels at his side, their own swords equally fast. When they burst out of the door, the ground was littered with bodies, both their side and the enemy's. Talon looked around, seeing only Caelians and Terstens standing, the three rebels at his side. He lowered his sword, a grin erupting as he turned to Lyle.

"Looks like it wasn't a good day to die after all."

Lyle threw back his head and laughed. "Our First Officer and General are going to want to know about this. Looks like it might be time to take care of the Prilonians once and for all."

Talon stared at Lyle. "The Caelians have a First Officer and my people have a General."

Lyle nodded. "That makes sense. It's the way it's always been done amongst our people. Ever since our two races originally became allies centuries ago."

"Talon!"

He looked up to see Brianne run towards him. She stopped in front of him, her gaze travelling over him. "You hurt?"

"I'm fine."

"You won't be soon," she muttered as she grabbed hold of his free hand and dragged him towards the trees.

"What did I do?"

Brianne didn't answer until they were amongst the trees. "Don't you ever leave me behind again. How can I protect your back if you take off like that? Next time you take me with you."

Talon nodded, sheathing his sword.

She jabbed a finger at his chest. "I'm serious."

"I know. I'll take you with me."

"Good." Her glare faded. "Now how about you show me how happy you are we're alive?"

Talon stared at her a moment before the meaning of her words sank in. He took a step closer, a slow grin forming. "It might take a while. I'm very happy we're both alive." His hands rested on her hips as he stared down at her.

"We could always stick with my method if you want."

"Not likely." His lips met hers as he pulled her close, an arm sliding around her back. His wings stretched out around them as he deepened the kiss.

"Enough of that."

The sharp words brought Talon's head up and he looked past Brianne to find Briant glaring at him, a bow in one hand. He guessed he should be glad it wasn't aimed at him. Keeping one arm around Brianne, he took a step forward. "Sir." He added a respectful nod.

"The rebels you found are off to spread the news about our arrival to their people," Briant said.

"Did we lose many soldiers?" Brianne asked.

"Not as many as the Prilonians. At the most we lost a handful at each garrison. We took out every one of their soldiers. Not a single one escaped."

"What next?" Talon asked.

"We wait until the leaders of the rebels can meet with us."

"What about the Holy City?" Brianne asked.

Talon felt the tension in Brianne and looked down at her. "What's wrong?"

She met his gaze. "I think that's where they take the Caelians to remove their wings before they send them over here as slaves."

Briant swore. "Under our noses. We need to deal with it soon. We'll talk to the rebels and see if they can keep the Prilonians busy while we capture the Holy City." He started to turn away.

Talon thought of the people still stuck at the capital of Terst. Some of them would be innocent. "What about the Tersten capital? When will the people there be rescued?"

"I don't know." Briant looked like he'd say more, then he shook his head and started to turn away.

"What happened?" Talon stepped forward, bringing Brianne with him. When Briant didn't answer, his words became a demand. "What happened?"

"I'm sorry, Talon."

He nearly reached out and shook the old man. Instead he asked calmly, "What happened?" Calm was the last thing he felt.

"Tell us," Brianne said.

Briant stared at his granddaughter a moment before his gaze returned to Talon. "The Prilonians executed hundreds of Terstens. They were hung from the wall of the Tersten capital. Your parents were among them."

Talon felt his hands curl into fists. He pulled away from Brianne. The ferocity of his people during the battle now made more sense. No wonder no Prilonians had survived. "Are there any Terstens left in the city?"

"We don't know."

He faced Briant, Brianne's hand against his back between his wings. "I want to fight. I don't care which battle, but I want to fight." The few Prilonians he'd killed didn't make up for all the lives they'd taken. "And what about the bodies?"

"There's plans to gather the dead tonight. Prilonian archers man the walls and it isn't safe to try during the day," Briant said.

Talon nodded. "I want to help."

"Me too," Brianne said.

Briant nodded, a short, sharp nod that reminded Talon of Brianne. "I'll arrange it. For now, we need to finish up here. We have to bury our dead, take care of the wounded and deal with the bodies of the enemy. Everyone is needed." Briant strode away without waiting for an answer.

Brianne continued to stand beside Talon, her hand on his back. "We'll make them pay. Not just for today, but also for the centuries they pitted us against each other and all the senseless deaths because of a war they created. We'll destroy them."

Maybe his parents had deserved to be hung, but how many of those on the wall had been innocent? How many had been tricked into thinking they were protecting their family, their people? Talon turned towards Brianne, his hand going behind her head as he tugged her close. "We'll destroy them. Together."

"Yes." Her arms went around him.

He remained there for a moment, taking comfort from her, his anger burning steadily. "Let's deal with everything here so we can return to Terst." He pulled away from her, taking her hand as they headed to the garrison.

It took the rest of the day to bury the dead, gather what arrows and bolts were still usable and see to the wounded. Even with soldiers left behind to protect the garrisons and officers remaining to talk with the leaders of the rebels, there were many soldiers who returned to the Tersten encampment.

As they waited for dark, the crowd waiting to collect the dead from the walls around the Tersten capital began to overflow the encampment. They were divided into four groups, one for each side of the city. And each of those groups was divided again for sections of the wall. Talon stared at the people in his group, Lyle, along with a large group of rebels who had chosen to join the mission, Bellamy, Brianne and three Caelians he hadn't met before. Of them all, he only trusted Brianne to watch his back. Not that it mattered. He was still going ahead with the mission. His anger at the Prilonians had only increased while he'd waited for this moment.

The call came to head out and Talon carried Brianne while Lyle carried Bellamy. The group flew towards their section of the wall, leaving Brianne, Bellamy and one of the Caelians to cover them while they flew in to collect the four bodies they'd been assigned.

Shouts rang out from the top of the walls and arrows whistled past him. Talon reached his target, wrapping his arm around the woman, his dagger slicing through the rope that held her there, her stiff cold body difficult to hold. Then he was flying back to camp, wishing he didn't have to leave Brianne to make her own way back, trying not to think about the woman in his arms. She could have been his sister. If Brianne hadn't involved Garnet in rescuing him, this woman could have easily been his sister. The thought caused fear to race through him.

As soon as he dropped the body in the camp, he

headed towards the city to look for Brianne. He swore when he found her shadowy figure still returning fire at the archers on the wall, all the other soldiers around her doing the same.

Dropping beside her, he grabbed his crossbow from his back, where it hung down low between his wings, and joined her. "Are you crazy? The order was to return."

Brianne flashed him a grin. "I guess that means you're crazy too."

He barely saw the grin in the shadows. "You've got no cover."

"We don't need it. We aren't lit up like idiots."

He had to admit the soldiers on the wall were clearly lit by the torches placed around them. A trumpet call sounded from their encampment. Not a single soldier moved. Again the call rang out.

Talon turned at the sound of wings behind him.

"Don't fire," Lyle's voice came out of the dark. He landed beside them. "The officers have returned and they're livid their orders aren't being followed." He laughed when the trumpet call came again and no one moved.

"I saw a young child up on that wall," Bellamy said.

"I did too," Brianne said.

Talon swore as fury hit him. Killing children

wasn't right. He aimed at another soldier, fierce satisfaction filling him when the man fell. "If others saw, no one will leave until this city is taken."

"It will be, but we're taking it from the inside. The officers have a plan and I was sent to fetch you," Lyle said.

Bellamy lowered his crossbow. "The tunnels into the House of the Lord and Lady. They'll be guarded."

"Yes. It's probably a suicide mission, but I did say it was a good day to die," Lyle said.

Talon returned his crossbow to his back. "I'm in."

"You're not leaving me behind," Brianne said.

"Or me," Bellamy said.

"Then let's go. Need a lift, dirt walker?" Lyle grinned at Bellamy, using the name that Talon and Conal regularly called him.

"If you think you can manage, bird-boy." Bellamy continued to hold his crossbow.

Still holding her bow, Brianne pressed her back against Talon's chest. "Ready when you are."

He wrapped his arms around her, wishing she wasn't coming with him, but glad she'd be at his side. "Let's take the city back."

Chapter Forty-Three

Brianne

Brianne crouched beside Talon, Bellamy pressed against her other side, waiting to invade the Tersten capital. Her bow was drawn back, an arrow ready to be fired the moment the word was given. She just needed light to see the target. Then the Prilonians would see what happened to those who tried to enslave her people and kill innocent Terstens.

She watched as a flaming arrow flew through the air and the command was given to attack. The flames momentarily lit up the guards at the hidden entrance leading to the House of the Lord and Lady and within seconds they were riddled with arrows and bolts. Brianne raced through the night with the rest of the soldiers. Amongst them were the three rebels, Marshall and Conal. She didn't know the other soldiers with them that were a mix of Caelians, Terstens and rebels.

Conal attacked the door, which was hidden inside a shallow natural cave, with his axe. Lanterns were lit and they were soon racing along a corridor, attacking the clusters of guards throughout it.

Brianne winced when one of their men fell, pierced by an arrow to his side. When she would have stopped to help him, he waved her on, clutching where the arrow was imbedded. With a nod she obeyed, continuing along the corridor with the rest of the group.

No one spoke, only fought, and soon they were breaking through the door at the other end of the tunnel, coming up into the lower levels of the House of the Lord and Lady. Brianne put away her bow, drawing her sword like those around her. The clash of steel filled the night as they fought their way through the corridor, headed for the stairs. Then they were in the street and under fire.

Brianne's gaze darted everywhere, trying to locate all threats. She crouched against one of the shrubs at the front of the House along with the rest of the team, who had spread out across the street.

"Get to the front gates. We have to get them open," one of the soldiers called from where he knelt behind a shrub to the side of the House, his bow drawn to take out enemy that fired on them.

Brianne raced at Talon's side, Bellamy and Marshall keeping up with them. Bellamy pulled ahead and Brianne made the decision she dreaded making. "Talon. Fly. Don't wait for me." She would only slow him down.

"I–"

"Fly! Get the gates." She veered off in another direction. "Bellamy. Marshall. Come on." She headed for the tallest building that should have a view of the gates, not waiting to see if anyone followed.

Talon took to the air, Conal, the rebels and the Caelians at his side. She prayed they'd make it. Her sword slashed at the soldiers who tried to keep her out of the building, Marshall and Bellamy beside her, several Terstens joining them. They raced through the nearly empty building and Brianne thought fleetingly of those who had once lived here, hoping they'd escaped and not been hung from the walls.

On the top floor, she broke a window to stare at the gate, her bow ready. She saw a movement and fired as soon as she was certain it wasn't one of their own.

Talon and his companions landed at the gate and Brianne fired on the soldiers who came out to attack.

Bellamy, Marshall and the soldiers who had followed her hung out the now broken windows also firing at those who tried to stop the gates from being opened.

"Hurry," Brianne muttered under her breath as she saw twenty Prilonians running for the gate. There was no way they could survive that many. She kept firing on the enemy, barely able to draw breath as she waited for the gate to be opened. "Hurry," she muttered again.

The gate swung open and she shouted in victory, those with her echoing the shout, none of them pausing in their attacks. Their people poured through the front gate in time to meet the arriving enemy. Relief rushed through Brianne when Talon was out of extreme danger. As much as she wanted to join him, she'd be able to protect him better from up here, picking off the enemy before most of them got close.

More of their people poured in the front gate and dawn found their army exhausted, but victorious. Brianne raced through the building, headed for Talon's side, wanting to make sure he wasn't hurt. Those who had followed her earlier followed her once again.

Upon reaching Talon, she threw herself at him, her bow still in one hand. Her lips met his and she ignored Conal's growl. Pulling back, she eyed him. "You're unharmed?"

Talon nodded. "Only a few scratches."

"If I tell you I was harmed, will I get that sort of treatment?" Lyle asked.

Her arms still around Talon, Brianne looked Lyle over. "I don't see anything."

He turned his back to her, his wings retracted. "Now can you see?"

There was a shallow cut across the middle of his back, but that barely kept her attention since it was such a minor wound. Her gaze was drawn to the ridges on his shoulder blades and the scars that ran the length of each of them. "What happened to your wings?"

Lyle faced her. "What do you mean?"

"The old scars on the ridges of your wings."

"I would have thought you'd know, being an Erien without wings."

"Know what? And what's an Erien?" She dropped one arm from around Talon so she could face Lyle.

"An Erien is a Caelian of mixed heritage, named after the first child born of Caelian and Tersten parentage," Lyle said.

"And the scars," Brianne prompted when he didn't continue.

"Erien bones often grow over where their wings would form. We've been operating on them for about a hundred years. We scrape the bone away so the wings can form. It doesn't work for every Erien. Some don't have the wing growth develop at all, but it doesn't hurt to check." He grinned. "Well, it does hurt, but it won't kill you."

"Both my parents are Caelians."

"Might have been one of your ancestors before they left Iralen to cross the Feronian Mountains."

Brianne could only stare at him, dazed. "Who does the operation? How do they know how to do it?" The question she really wanted to ask, she couldn't bring herself to voice. Can I have the operation?

"Our doctors perform it, but you're out of action for about a month if you've got no wings and up to a year if you have wings. You have to take it easy while they develop properly."

"And anyone can have this operation?" Brianne couldn't take her gaze off Lyle as she waited for the answer.

"Anyone who's willing to give it a try," Lyle said. "Even you."

Brianne felt light headed. She could get wings. She could fly without help.

Talon's arm tightened around her. "Does anyone die from this operation?"

"The last death was about sixty years ago. We don't take unnecessary risks with the lives of our people," Lyle said. "But it isn't a guarantee of wings. Sometimes there are none and sometimes even if there are wings they don't grow no matter what is done."

She wasn't certain if she completely trusted the rebels, but her people would look out for her while she was incapacitated. Talon would too. "When we've taken back Iralen I want to talk to one of your doctors." Almost anything was worth a try if it meant wings. Hope mixed with scepticism. Maybe.

Lyle nodded. Before he could say anything else, a Caelian dropped out of the sky to land at their feet. "First Officer wishes to see you." He faced Brianne.

Bellamy, who had followed her, said, "You're not leaving me out of anything." He turned to Lyle. "Want to give me a lift, bird-boy?"

"Sure, dirt walker. Let's hope it's about killing a few more Prilonians."

Chapter Forty-Four

Talon

Talon leaned against a wall in a room that had been taken over in the fortress for discussions. Brianne was seated next to Marshall and Bellamy leaned against the wall in the opposite corner. The room was crowded, many of the people he recognised from fighting along side them. This hadn't been what he'd expected of the summons. At the front of the room, the officers sat facing the crowd.

Briant held up his hand for silence. He rose from the stool he sat on, officers from his army and those of the Terstens on either side of him, rebel leaders mixed in amongst them. "We're looking for squads and units willing to volunteer to help us take the Holy City, entering through the hidden passages. Today we learned Elden, the impostor Supreme One, left before the city was locked down. He organised the taking of the Tersten capital before he retreated to the Holy City."

The moment the crowd realised Elden would be at the Holy City, those seated rose and many called out. The noise was a swell of sound. Talon stepped away from the wall, wanting to be amongst those who captured Elden. He might not have been the only one to mistreat their people, but he was the leader of them on this side of the Feronian Mountains.

Briant held up his hand again for silence. This time it took longer for everyone to settle. They all remained standing. "That isn't the only task we have that we need volunteers for. We need enough squads and units to hit the eight defensive towers around our ancestor's capital city, Taeranelle, so our relatives in Iralen can destroy the Prilonians. We need Caelians to carry Wildfire and Terstens to provide cover for them and set it alight once it has been dropped on the towers." Again Briant held up a hand. "I want you all to realise this is the most dangerous task of all. There is no way to put Wildfire out. It will even burn under water."

Talon's gaze was drawn to Brianne as she turned to speak to Conal who had joined her. Like the rest of the crowd, they were both still standing. Brianne nodded then raised her hand. Talon pushed through the crowd, raising his own hand as he stopped between Brianne and Marshall.

"You don't have to do this," Brianne said. "You don't know how dangerous Wildfire is. It's like carrying death."

"You're not leaving me behind." Talon met her blue eyes, seeing worry and determination in them. He wondered if she could see the same in his. "Besides, someone has to show you they're glad you survived."

Brianne grinned, facing the front of the room, moving closer so her side pressed against his, her arm still raised. "Maybe we'll even get lucky enough not to be interrupted."

Talon sent a glare to Conal when he snickered. The glare became a look of annoyance when he noticed Bellamy's hand was also raised. That was all he needed. Couldn't he find someone else to pester?

"Do you mind if I attack the Holy City?" Marshall asked Talon. "I want to be there when they get Elden."

"You do what you have to. I'll keep an eye out for your sister when we attack the Prilonians," Talon said.

"Thanks." Marshall turned his attention back to the front of the room.

Talon did the same, lowering his hand when the order was given to separate into two groups. Those attacking the Holy City left the room, more than three quarters of the crowd and most of the leaders.

"What made you volunteer?" Talon asked Brianne as they moved towards the front of the room.

"Conal said Grandad asked me to help. He wants as many people as possible who have handled Wildfire to be involved in the attack." Brianne sat on one of the stools at the front of the room, Conal and Bellamy sitting on the other side of her.

Talon sat beside Brianne. "What's it like?"

Brianne nodded towards Briant who was handed a leather bag. "I think you're about to find out."

Three men brought in a large metal trough and placed it in front of Briant. Wood was placed inside and two pails were placed beside him. One of water and one of sand.

Briant removed a glass globe from the leather bag. "Wildfire." He moved the globe from side to side and the liquid within sloshed around, a murky grey filling nine tenths of the globe. He held it over the trough and beckoned two men forward who held a heavy blanket around the trough. Once it was in place, he dropped the globe and stepped well back. The men tipped the blanket into one end of the trough.

"What did he do that for?" Talon asked.

"To catch any splashes when it broke. It burns for days and there's no way to put it out," Brianne said.

"There has to be some way. What's it made of?"

Brianne shrugged.

As soon as everyone was out of the way, Briant took a bow and lit an arrow, firing it into the trough. It went up in a whoosh of sound and flames. Once the initial burst had settled, Briant stepped forward and tipped first water and then sand over the fire. Neither made a difference. Sound travelled around the room as people spoke in hushed tones.

Talon stared at the flames that hadn't changed, still eating hungrily through the wood, nothing left of the blanket. "Why didn't you ever use that against us?" His people wouldn't have had a chance.

"Because it spreads easily and there's no way to stop it."

"Why now?" Talon couldn't take his gaze from the flames.

"I don't know," Brianne said.

"I do." Conal leaned forward so Talon could see him around Brianne. "The defensive towers have nothing near them and only Prilonian soldiers are ever allowed to enter them or be around them. There'll be no civilian casualties."

Talon was finally able to drag his gaze from the Wildfire. "What about the rest of their army? How do we get rid of them?"

"The towers are their barracks. They've made protecting them their priority so no one can take the city in the same way they did," Conal said.

"So we take out the towers and the city is left vulnerable."

Conal nodded.

"Then what happens?" Talon asked.

"The rebels attack and any of our people who survive the attack on the defensive towers join them," Conal said.

"And this has a chance to work?" Talon asked.

"Yes." Conal's gaze momentarily fell on Brianne. "Do you think Briant would ask his own granddaughter to volunteer if he didn't think they'd win?"

Talon thought of his parents. "I have no idea."

"He wouldn't," Brianne said. "Not unless we had at least a seventy percent success rate. Below those odds wouldn't be acceptable."

"He sent you into the heart of Terst," Talon pointed out.

Brianne grinned. "He calculated that at ninety-eight percent. I guess your defences weren't as good as you thought they were."

Talon shook his head. "No one else could have got through them." He met her gaze. "Any of them."

She continued to grin, turning back to face the front of the room, her hand reaching for his.

Talon linked his fingers through Brianne's, his gaze returning to the flames that continued to burn brightly. Briant stood near the flames as he answered questions. The Prilonians were about to find out what happened to those who messed with his people. It might be centuries coming, but it wasn't going to be pretty. He thought of the woman he'd cut free from the wall. The Prilonians didn't deserve pretty.

Chapter Forty-Five

Brianne

Brianne couldn't stop thinking of the two globes of Wildfire that were in a pouch at her waist. They were pressed against her stomach while Talon flew her above the forested land below them, headed for the rebel army that was camped outside Taeranelle. It had taken them two days to cross both the Feronian Mountains and the land between them and the rebel army. Now they were less than an hour from their destination.

Conal flew with them, carrying Bellamy. Lyle and his two companions were also with them, each carrying Terstens. There were also nearly a hundred soldiers, half of them Caelians, half Terstens. It would have taken the Caelians less time to travel the distance if they hadn't carried Terstens and needed regular breaks.

Brianne's grip tightened on her bow as she fought the urge to check on the globes again. Not far from her she saw Bellamy's hand brush against the pouch at his waist and she felt a tiny measure of relief that she wasn't the only one worried about carrying Wildfire.

When the signal was finally given to land, Brianne nearly cheered, then dread rushed through her as she worried over Talon's next landing. So far they hadn't crashed. None of them had been perfect landings, but it would be her own fault if anything went wrong since she'd been the one to turn down Conal's offer to carry her and chosen to go with Talon instead. She tensed as the ground came closer, an army spread out below them. She tried to focus on the soldiers instead of the ground coming closer. It was impossible. They landed in a stumble, both staying on their feet.

Brianne's empty hand went to the globes, brushing across them as she checked they were still intact. The globes felt smooth and unbroken through the leather pouch and she stepped away from Talon as he let her go.

"I'll be glad when this is over," Talon muttered. "I don't like the idea of you carrying Wildfire."

"I don't like the idea of you carrying it through a battle," Brianne said.

Talon grinned. "I'm not worried, I'll have you to watch out for me."

Brianne slung the bow on her back, hoping she didn't fail him. They had one chance. If they didn't destroy the defensive towers, there would be no retreat. The Prilonians would destroy them instead.

Lyle joined them. "Do you want something to eat? There's usually a cook pot of stew at the main campfire."

"No." Brianne shook her head. There was no way she'd be able to swallow even a mouthful. She'd probably be starving afterwards. Hopefully Lyle was right and there'd still be a pot of stew cooking once the battle was over.

Talon glanced at the sky. "What are our orders while we wait the couple of hours till the sun sets?"

"Make yourself at home. Relax," Lyle said.

Brianne was tempted to tell him he was an idiot if he thought she could relax. Her hands brushed across the globes again, unable to stop herself. But she wasn't the only one doing so. Many Terstens around her regularly did the same. And yet it would be the Caelians who had the most dangerous task. The Caelians and Talon.

When Lyle wandered away, Brianne turned to Talon. "You will be careful tonight."

"Stop worrying."

"Seventy percent chance of winning still means there's a thirty percent chance you won't make it."

Talon reached out and tugged her to his side, keeping his arm draped around her shoulders. "You focus on taking out any soldier who even looks like he might be thinking of attacking and I'll drop the Wildfire on the south-west tower as planned. We've got through worse."

"There would be nothing worse than being drenched in Wildfire and lit up. Your body would burn long after you were dead." Brianne shuddered at the thought.

"Everything will be fine." Talon spoke again, "Except for the Prilonians."

"I hope so."

They found somewhere quiet to sit and eventually Conal and Bellamy joined them. No one seemed to be interested in talking. They were tired from the journey and dozed fitfully until night fell. At the call to fall in, they gathered into the groups organised to attack each of the eight defensive towers while the rebel army prepared to attack in their wake.

Brianne pressed her back against Talon's chest, her

bow held tight in one hand, the other once again brushing across the globes. Talon launched into the air and Brianne tried to focus on the joy of flying. Fear and worry prevented it. She could focus on nothing but the attack ahead. Talon landed in bow sight of the tower while Bellamy and several other Terstens were dropped next to her.

She undid the pouch and handed the two globes to Talon. She started to step away from him, then came close instead. "Be careful." Her lips brushed across his before she stepped back, her grip tight on the bow.

"Just be ready to set the place on fire once we're out of the way." Talon launched into the air, five other Caelians joining him, including Conal.

Brianne readied her bow. A glance to her right showed Bellamy had his crossbow ready, and to her left four Terstens had their crossbows aimed at the tower. Behind them was a shaded lantern, ready for her to touch the specially prepared arrows to it so she could set fire to the tower.

Her gaze flicked between the shadows in the sky and the tower they aimed for. Then a shout rang out in the night and she let loose her first arrow, the second not far behind. She wasn't about to let the Prilonians get anywhere near the tower weapons. Not while Talon was headed straight for them.

Chapter Forty-Six

Talon

Talon held a globe in each hand, flying as fast as he could to the tower, the five Caelians spreading out in the sky around him in the hope that at least one of them would get through. He could feel the movement of the liquid inside the globes as he flew through the night sky, staying above the height of the defensive tower and hopefully out of friendly fire. The tower was lit with lanterns and so far not a single Prilonian had been able to get near the three overgrown crossbows in the south-west tower.

A slight smile formed as he thought of Brianne, on the ground, keeping him safe. It was hard to believe he trusted a Caelian with his life, but he did. He trusted her as much as he trusted Marshall and Garnet. The thought of his sister brought to mind the short time he'd spent with her the day before he'd left Terst. He'd taken her to see the trough of Wildfire, still burning that afternoon. It had chilled him to see those flames leap across the bottom of the empty trough, looking for something to devour and finding only metal. He had planned to show her that the Prilonians would soon be dealt with and out of their lives, but all he'd done was cause her to worry about his survival.

Talon swore as one of the Prilonians fired a tower weapon and he swerved out of the line of fire, nearly crashing into a Caelian. The Prilonian was quickly pierced by an arrow, only to be replaced by one of the many Prilonians now pouring into the top of the tower. It was going to be impossible for Brianne and the Terstens to take them out before there were casualties.

The air was filled with large bolts, but he wove his way past them, feeling the rush of metal as one passed close by. His grip tightened on the globes and he had to force himself to relax. He didn't want to break them before he reached the tower.

There was a roar as the Caelian to his left was hit and he tumbled from the sky. Talon fought against the urge to help the man. He continued to fly towards the tower. Then he was above it, a Prilonian was hanging out from under the edge of the roof that covered the open area at the top, firing his bow at them. Talon dropped one of the globes onto the roof, making sure he was high enough that the liquid didn't splash him. Around him he saw several of his companions do the same before they flew out of the way of the attacks.

An arrow grazed his side and he swerved to avoid another one, losing altitude. A couple of Prilonians fell out of the tower, bolts and arrows protruding from them. Talon tried to take aim to throw his last globe into the tower like he'd been ordered. It was impossible. There was a constant barrage of shots and he was forced to swerve, barely missing Conal.

Conal swore as his last globe was knocked from his hand to crash to the ground below. "I'll try and distract them. Get your globe in there." He flew at the tower, drawing his axe to swoop and dive at the Prilonians.

In the distance, one of the defensive towers went up in flames, a second one following. Only another six to go. Talon dived to the side. An arrow flew past him, far too close for comfort. Then he saw his opportunity as Conal cleared an edge of the tower.

Diving forward Talon tossed the globe in, yelling, "Leave. It's done."

"Twice done," a Caelian called from the other side of the tower.

"Follow." Conal shot into the sky, heading up and away from the tower.

A flare of light had Talon glancing behind him to see another tower go up in flames. He flew harder, wanting to get far enough away so Brianne could light up their tower. Another flare of light and this time when he checked behind him, he saw it was the south-west tower. Shouts sounded around him as another flaming arrow flew towards the tower, this one lighting the ground.

Talon grinned. The globe Conal had dropped hadn't been wasted after all. By the time he reached Brianne's side, there were only two towers left to destroy. Still grinning, he reached out for her, pulling her to him. "You happy we're alive?"

Brianne laughed. "Like you wouldn't believe."

He pressed his lips against hers, ignoring Conal's comment to break it up. When he drew back, his lips automatically formed a smile. "Ready to join the rebel army?"

Brianne shook her head. "Once all the towers are alight."

"You missed it," Conal said. "It was while you were pawing at each other." He looked from one to the other. "What am I meant to tell Officer Finnin when he asks me for a full report?"

Brianne grinned. "That there was a great deal of gratitude for our survival?" She turned to Talon. "Let's join the rebel army and finish taking back Taeranelle."

"Sounds good to me." He pulled her close when she turned her back to him, holding her tight, relieved they'd both survived the first part of the plan.

Talon didn't think anything could be as hard as what they'd already survived. He was only partly correct. When the rebels descended on Taeranelle, the Prilonians' first response was to fight, but everything soon broke down into confusion. Slaves ran from the city and got in the way of the fighting. Civilian Prilonians joined the soldiers that still lived, fighting for their homes. And fires sprang up in the city, but unlike Wildfire they could be doused with some effort.

Early morning brought with it a clear view of the havoc the rebels had brought to Taeranelle. The dead lay in the streets along with the wounded. Civilians sobbed and pleaded as they were rounded up and the last of the soldiers were incarcerated until their fate could be decided.

Talon stood beside Brianne, his sword in his hand

as he surveyed the city. Brianne shifted her sword to her left hand so she could lean against his left side. He reached out to put an arm around her waist, drawing her closer, exhaustion dragging at him. "If I'd known how good you were with a dagger, I would have insisted you hand yours over the morning you cut the rope I tied you with." She had fought with her sword and throwing darts and when she'd used up all the darts, pulled out her dagger to use with her sword.

Brianne smiled fleetingly. "I wouldn't have given it up."

Talon's gaze searched the area again. "I didn't see Marshall's sister anywhere."

"I didn't realise there'd be so many people." Brianne took another slow look at the part of the city where they stood.

Lyle strode towards them, a bow in one hand, stopping beside them in the middle of the street. "This is only the beginning. There are other cities to be taken back. But they'll be easy now Taeranelle has fallen. The majority of the army was here." He looked them over. "Glad to see the pair of you made it through mostly unharmed."

"I am too." Brianne turned to Talon with a grin. "How about you? I haven't noticed you showing me you're happy we're alive."

"Maybe it's your turn to show me, but how about you stick with my method?"

Brianne laughed, but before she could do anything else, Conal dropped out of the sky to land near them. "Officer Finnin needs the two of you."

Talon groaned. "He has the worst timing."

"Yep, but too bad." Brianne reached up to slide a hand around his neck, pulling him towards her with a grin. "He can wait, gratitude can't." She pressed her lips against his and he held her tight, not caring for the moment what Briant wanted.

Chapter Forty-Seven

Brianne

Brianne looked around the small room Conal had brought them to. "Where's my grandad?" It was the foyer of a house that seemed to have missed most of the fighting.

"Here." Conal held out a letter.

"Wasn't he organising the attack on the Holy City?" Brianne took the letter, not even glancing at it. "Have they attacked yet?"

Conal gestured towards the letter. "Read it if you want an explanation."

She stared at Conal a moment longer before she decided she wouldn't get any information from him. She read the first paragraph, turning to Talon with a grin, relief rushing through her. "They've taken the Holy City. Zinervie and the other two with her are safe and still have their wings." She reached for his hand, her grin firmly in place.

"That was all he wanted?" Talon looked from Brianne to Conal. "I thought you said he wanted to see us."

"Read the rest of it." Conal gestured towards the letter Brianne still held.

"I can't believe she's safe. I want to see her." She couldn't stop grinning, relief making her feel almost giddy.

"Read the letter." There was a sharpness to Conal's tone.

Brianne sent Conal a half hearted glare, the effect ruined by her grin. "All right. Don't be so impatient. Let me have a moment to celebrate." She turned back to the letter, her grin evaporating the moment she read the next paragraph.

"What is it? What's wrong?" Talon reached for the letter.

Brianne dropped her hand to her side, crumpling the letter in her fist. "Elden escaped. He had his own personal escape tunnel and left his people behind to cover his retreat. He's headed towards the mountains. Grandad wants us to join a group of people Conal is organising to hunt Elden down." She was tired, desperate for sleep and could only imagine Talon felt the same.

Talon nodded. He turned to Conal. "When are we leaving?"

"In about half an hour. I've gathered most of the people already. Bellamy and Lyle will join us along with a handful of Caelians. We'll be moving fast. Have something to eat, get cleaned up and I'll meet you back here," Conal said.

At the reminder of food, Brianne's stomach growled. "Eating sounds like a good idea." Particularly since she hadn't been able to eat before the attack on the towers. "But we need sleep too."

"No time for resting now. There'll be regular breaks where you can have a nap. The rebels have food and medical help set up at the front gate. Don't take too long," Conal warned.

Brianne wanted to argue. Instead, with a nod, she headed outside. Talon walked beside her and she looked up at him. "I can't believe he got away." She threw her letter into a burning house they passed further down the street. "We've got to capture him. He can't continue to escape."

"We'll get him. There must be nowhere left for him to hide."

Brianne nodded as they reached the front gates. "I hope not." She stifled a yawn.

It didn't take them long to eat, have Talon's wounds attended to and head back to the house where they were to meet Conal, finding Bellamy there too. They were introduced to the Caelians that were to join them and were soon soaring through the sky towards the Feronian Mountains. Brianne was passed between Talon and Conal at each short rest stop and they reached a garrison by midday where a message awaited them.

Leaning against Talon, Brianne watched as Conal read the message, crumpling it and throwing it back to the boy who'd given it to him. "Burn it." He turned to the group watching him. "First Officer Ewyn is leading a group that has been tracking Elden from the Holy City. They believe he's now headed for the coast. Somewhere around the border. They'll leave a message at the Tersten capital to let us know if there's any change in direction and where they'll send the next message." Conal's wings snapped out. "Let's go."

Brianne bit back a groan, wanting to demand they rest longer. She looked up at Talon. He looked as exhausted as she felt. Holding her bow, she turned her back to Talon, waiting for him to wrap his arms around her.

"We need to go faster." Talon pulled her against him.

"What we really need is a rest."

"No, we need to be there when Elden is found."

She wanted to argue his words. But she couldn't. Elden had to be stopped and she wanted to be among the ones who caught him. "Yes." She felt his arms tighten around her before he shot into the air.

Talon headed down the side of the mountain, aiming for the capital, pulling out ahead of everyone. "I'm going to sleep for a week when this is over."

She was tempted to agree, but a week was a long time. Especially after years of waiting. "No you're not. You're going to keep an eye on the doctors so they don't mess up my operation."

"You're going through with it?"

Brianne tilted her head so she could see Talon. "Yes."

Talon remained silent a moment before he answered. "I'll keep an eye on them."

They fell silent as they continued through the skies, Talon keeping up the faster pace, the others matching him. When they reached the capital, Conal collected the new message and told them nothing had changed.

They were still headed for the coast. After a short rest, Conal strode to Brianne, waited for her to rise and turn her back to him so he could carry her into the sky.

Late evening found them taking a break at a farmhouse several hours from the coast. They gathered at a timber table set under a tree in the house yard, a lantern and the full moon lighting the table. Brianne ate the meal the farmers provided, sitting beside Talon who looked worn out. She reached out to rest the back of her hand against his cheek, relieved to find his skin a normal temperature.

"What?" Talon took her hand from his cheek, holding onto it.

"You look wrecked."

"It's been a long day." He shot a look across the table at Bellamy. "But I guess it's better than being carried."

Bellamy laughed. "Don't worry Talon, when you're too exhausted to do anything but fall at Elden's feet I'll take care of him for you."

"Watch it, dirt walker," Lyle said. "I might accidentally let you go next time we take to the sky together."

"Enough talk," Conal said. "We have three hours

rest before we head out again. The quicker you eat, the longer you get to sleep."

Silence descended and the meal was rapidly finished. They were shown to a barn and given blankets to help make the hay more comfortable. Brianne spread her blanket out next to Talon's, falling instantly asleep the moment she lay down near him.

When Conal shook her awake, Brianne groaned, looking blearily up at him. "I'm awake," she muttered when he continued to shake her shoulder.

"Then get up. We need to move before Elden disappears."

Brianne struggled to sit up, hearing Talon groan from beside her as he sat up too. "Surely he can't have covered as much ground as we have."

Conal ignored her comment, talking to Talon. "Your turn to carry Brianne."

Talon nodded and rose to his feet as Conal left the barn. "Come on. We'll be at the coast before daybreak at this speed. Once Elden is caught we can focus on trying to get you your own wings." Holding out a hand to Brianne he grinned. "I swear you're gaining weight by the hour."

Grabbing her bow, Brianne swatted his hand away with a halfhearted glare. "Or you're getting weaker by the hour." Rising, she strode ahead of him as they headed outside.

Talon reached her side. "Not likely. Turn around so we can get this over with."

Hearing the exhaustion in his voice, Brianne stopped and reached up to check his temperature again, relieved his skin still felt cool.

"I'm well. Stop worrying."

"You've been pushing yourself. Of course I'm going to worry."

Conal bellowed, "Everyone in the air. Time's wasting."

"Turn around," Talon said again.

She held her hand against his cheek a moment longer before she turned away, pressing her back against him. "The only thing keeping me awake is the thought of putting an arrow in Elden."

Talon leapt into the air, taking Brianne with him. "Don't make it a killing shot, I want him to feel my bolt too."

"Deal."

When they were still a couple of hours from the coast, they caught sight of a squad to their left, also headed for the coast. They changed their direction, catching up with them before they all landed on the ground.

"Zinervie." Brianne raced towards her friend the moment Talon let her go. She wrapped her arms around her, relieved when Zinervie's arms did the same.

"I'm so sorry," Zinervie said. "I'm the worst friend ever." She pulled back slightly. "Who is that?"

Brianne turned to see Talon behind her, watching Zinervie. She smiled at him, letting him know she was safe. She took a step away from Zinervie. "This is Talon."

"Talon." Marshall pushed past the rest of the squad to join them. "I'm glad you'll be with me when we take Elden down."

"No killing him," Ewyn ordered, reaching their group. "We'll leave you behind if you can't remember to keep your promise."

"I won't. I want to, but I won't." Marshall turned to Talon. "Did you see my sister?"

Talon shook his head. "No. Sorry. Maybe she wasn't in Taeranelle. There's other cities. She could be at one of them."

"Maybe."

Brianne could see the disappointment and worry on Marshall's face. "We'll help you find her."

Ewyn spoke to Brianne before Marshall could

answer her. "You're unharmed? Ailis told me I was to check on you the moment I saw you." He grinned.

Brianne fleetingly answered his grin with one of her own, knowing he hadn't taken his sister's concerns seriously. "I'm fine." Exhausted and needing more than a few hours sleep, but he wasn't interested in hearing that. "I can't wait to catch Elden. We are allowed to shoot him, aren't we? As long as it's not a lethal shot."

"Legs or arms only if necessary, but no filling his limbs with arrows so that he bleeds to death. We need him alive to question him," Ewyn said. "Time to go. I want to catch them before they reach the coast."

"Them?" Brianne turned so her back was to Talon.

"My turn." Conal walked over to them as Talon started to wrap his arms around Brianne.

Brianne nodded, stepping away from Talon so Conal could carry her. "Uncle Ewyn? Them?"

"The tracks we're following are from four different horses." Ewyn shot into the air. "Hurry up. Day is coming."

Chapter Forty-Eight

Talon

As much as he would have hated to say it, Talon was glad it was Conal's turn to carry Brianne. He was utterly exhausted and glad he could see the coast in the distance. He flew beside Conal, keeping an eye on Brianne.

"I see something," one of the Caelians called out, pointing off into the distance.

Talon looked to where he pointed, seeing a cloud of dust hanging in the air, a figure on horseback, three horses trailing behind him on lead ropes. Exhaustion fell away as adrenaline hit him and he increased his speed, like his companions did. They were soon close enough for Talon to see Elden, the hood of his black robe thrown back, glancing over his shoulder, setting free his extra horses.

"He's headed for a boat. Don't let him near it," Ewyn called out.

Talon grabbed his crossbow, readying it as he continued to fly towards Elden, trying to keep up with the speed of the Caelians. They were slightly ahead of him, but he let off the first shot. The bolt flew past Elden, who tried to get more speed from his horse as arrows rained down around him. One arrow grazed the horse who reared, throwing Elden to the ground.

He was instantly on his feet, running to the rowboat pulled up on the shore, trying to push it towards the sea. He barely managed to get it to move before he was surrounded. Talon kept his crossbow trained on Elden, fighting the urge to shoot the man in front of him. Now his feet were on the ground he'd have better aim.

An arrow struck Elden. "Whoops," Brianne said, her tone sounding anything but apologetic.

Talon momentarily grinned, even more tempted to shoot Elden. He stared at the man who had caused so much pain for their people. The black robed man was light skinned with sandy brown hair and hazel eyes. An ordinary man who looked more like someone who'd help people rather than send them into slavery.

Ewyn pointed to a handful of soldiers. "Check the

ship that's waiting offshore." He turned to Elden. "Taeranelle has fallen and we're helping the rebels take back Iralen. Where did you think you were going to hide?"

"Prilonia. They'll send ships to recapture Iralen. You're fools if you think being at war with my people will be any better than fighting each other," Elden sneered.

Talon couldn't help it. He shot Elden in the leg before he stopped to think about it. The man roared, staggering.

"Hold your fire." Ewyn held up a hand.

"Fighting in a real war is better than being tricked into a fake one regardless of what we face," Talon said.

Elden laughed. "You're a fool. Even your father thought so." He looked around at the soldiers who encircled him. "You're all fools."

Talon's hands tightened on his crossbow, but a look from Ewyn kept him from firing another bolt at Elden.

Two of the Caelians who had gone to check out the ship, flew back swiftly, remaining in the air as one of them spoke. "They're firing on us, sir."

"Looks like it's already begun," Elden said, a smug smile forming.

Ewyn raised his fist as he launched across the short distance to Elden, knocking him to the ground, continuing to hover. "Brianne, Marshall, Bellamy. Take care of the prisoner. Everyone else to the ship." He rose into the air, heading out to sea.

Talon shared a look with Brianne before he followed Ewyn, wishing he could take her with him. His last glimpse of the three of them was Brianne and Marshall keeping their bow and crossbow trained on Elden while Bellamy tied him up.

As they flew, Ewyn split them into groups, giving them orders about the direction they were to attack from. Talon was put in the group that was ordered to land and attack with swords. That suited him. He was much better with a sword.

"Kill where necessary, subdue where possible," Ewyn said before the groups separated to attack.

Talon quickly reached the ship, the sailors returning fire with their bows. He slung his crossbow on his back, out of the way of his wings and drew his sword as he landed, attacking the nearest sailor. It didn't take him long to realise that hovering as he attacked was better than trying to work with the rolling movement of the deck and he put into practice some of the moves Brianne had taught him about fighting with wings.

The early morning was filled with shouted orders, cries of pain, the ring of metal and the thud of bodies on the deck. Talon swung his sword, able to put more force into his attacks with the help of his wings driving him forward. Energy sang through him as he fought one sailor after another, feeling alive. Completely focused on the sailor he fought and his immediate surroundings, it took him several minutes to realise the word truce was being called over and over again.

He held the point of his sword towards the sailor, his gaze scanning his surroundings. All around the deck sailors began to drop their weapons, hands raised above their heads.

"Tie them up," Ewyn ordered several soldiers. "The rest of you keep your weapons at the ready."

As soon as the sailors were tied up, Ewyn ordered half his soldiers back to shore. Talon was relieved he was one of them. He wanted to make sure Brianne was safe. Conal was also sent back.

Talon landed beside Brianne, smiling when he found her with her bow still trained on Elden. The man wasn't going anywhere. He was well tied and lay on his side in the dirt, glaring at Brianne. "Your uncle will be upset with you if you kill him."

"I'm not planning to shoot him." She paused a moment. "But accidents do occasionally happen."

"I'll swear it was an accident," Marshall offered.

"Put your bow away," Conal said to Brianne before turning to the soldiers beside him. "See if you can round up the horses that escaped." Then he faced Brianne. "Find shelter where we can take a break before we return to the capital."

"Which capital?" Talon asked.

"The Caelian one," Conal said.

Bellamy joined the conversation. "The Caelians aren't the only ones who have a claim on him." He indicated Elden with a sharp gesture from his hand. "We deserve the right to help decide what happens to him too."

"We're discussing locations for a permanent meeting place on the border, but for now, our capital is secure and closest. The Tersten leaders will get to have their say regarding Elden," Conal said.

Brianne slid her hand into Talon's. "You want to help me find shelter before this conversation turns into a political argument?"

Talon nodded. "Sure." He felt too exhausted to say more and almost envied Bellamy's lack of exhaustion. Thinking of his recent fight, Talon smiled. No, he didn't envy Bellamy's lack of wings. He'd never fought better.

"What are you thinking about?" Brianne asked as they left the group behind, several Caelians and Marshall joining the heated discussion.

"Wings."

Brianne stopped walking to stare up at him, returning his smile. "I'm right, aren't I? They're worth it."

Images flickered through his mind. Instead of the usual pain filled ones he associated with his wings, they included having his arms wrapped around Brianne as he carried her. Fighting with the advantage of the power of his wings. Crossing the land at an unbelievable speed. "Yes. They are." He turned back in the direction they'd been walking. "Let's find some shelter so we can have a rest then take Elden to somewhere more secure. I don't like how open and unprotected we are here."

Brianne nodded. "No point in taking unnecessary chances." She picked up her pace.

Talon nearly asked her to slow down, but he forced himself to match her speed. Not long now and he could take a rest.

Chapter Forty-Nine

Brianne

Brianne followed the guard to the cell where Macklyn was kept. Upon returning Elden to the Caelian capital yesterday, she'd asked if she could talk to Macklyn. Word had finally been brought to her that she could.

The guard stopped to unlock another gate and followed her through before he locked it behind them. She was tempted to ask how many more gates there were, but she guessed if it kept prisoners from escaping, what did it matter?

The guard opened yet another gate, but this time, he didn't follow her through. "Fifth cell on the right." He gestured in the direction before he closed the gate and locked it.

Brianne slowly turned to face the direction he had

indicated, taking a single step forward. She hadn't expected to be locked in here too. A glance over her shoulder showed the guard had his back to her, his hand resting on the hilt of his sword where it hung at his side. She continued along the corridor, looking in cells as she passed, counting the ones on the right. They were empty. She stopped in front of the only one with an occupant. He sat on the narrow bed fixed to the wall on the left side of the cell, leaning against the wall, his wings retracted. To the right of him was an enclosed area with a closed door, the rest of the cell empty.

Macklyn remained on his bed, the sheet and light blanket a rumpled heap at his feet. "They said you wanted to see me. Did you come to gloat?"

She shook her head. "Why did you tell Elden where I was?" Ewyn had told her Elden had returned to Terst because of what Macklyn had told him.

"He asked where you were."

"You were told to tell no one."

Macklyn rose to his feet, stalking to the bars that separated them. "He wasn't no one. He was the Supreme One. When he asks you a question, you answer. I'm locked in here because of you." He jabbed a finger in her direction.

"You're locked in here because you also told them I'd been caught."

"The Supreme One said to tell them that. He said that to tell them otherwise would have caused the death of many squads in a futile attempt to rescue you. The loss of that many lives wasn't worth trying to rescue one person just because of how important your family is."

"How could you believe him? My family would never have rescued me if it meant so many were to die. I wouldn't have expected it of them."

"You told the dirt walker he could kill me."

Her earlier anger at the slur against her family evaporated in a smile, she fought to contain, as she remembered Talon's comment. "I didn't. He just took my words that way."

"You're going to destroy our people. Not everyone believes the lies you've spread about the Holy Ones being impostors. Your family wanted to gain more control. That's what all this is about."

All sense of wanting to smile faded. "You're an idiot if you believe that. Who else believes you?"

Macklyn's lips slowly curved into a smile. "I'll get out of here one day. I was only following the orders of the Supreme One. His word is above law. His word is direct from the gods themselves."

"They won't let you out of here." Ewyn had told her that Macklyn went against orders and there was no way he was getting out.

"Sacred Law is above common law." He grasped one of the bars and moved as close to them as possible, lowering his voice. "And I'll make sure you pay for every moment I've spent in here."

Brianne wanted to take a step back at the venom in his tone and gaze. Instead she remained where she was. "They'll never let you out of here. I'll make certain they know you've threatened me."

"And like every other time, it'll be your word against mine."

Brianne recalled each time he'd managed to twist situations so they went in his favour. But not this time. This time he was behind bars and she was going to make certain he remained there. "My family will help keep you locked up. They'll believe me when I say you threatened me."

"Will they? When I've already voiced my concerns that this has all been a ruse to make things more difficult for me?" His tone changed to one that was a blend of uncertainty, sorrow and hope. "She wants to see me? Really? You can't imagine how badly I want to apologise to her after the Supreme One tricked me into betraying her. But how can I expect her to forgive me? She'll want to get even with me. How do I know this isn't a way to get even with me? Maybe even say I've threatened her."

Brianne could see the scene perfectly. How many times had he swayed someone to his thinking? "I'll tell them about the act you put on for them."

Macklyn laughed softly. "You do that. It doesn't matter. Of course I told you about my concerns when I begged your forgiveness. Do you want me to play that scene out for you? I bet I could even manage a tear or two."

This time Brianne did take a step back, wishing she hadn't bothered to come and ask her question. "I don't care what you say, I'll make sure you're locked up forever. You were an idiot to believe Elden."

"I would've done as he said even if I hadn't believed him." Macklyn glared at her a moment before he turned and took the several steps back to his bed. He faced her again, still standing. "A million times over." Sitting on the bed again, he leaned against the wall, stretching his legs out in front of him.

Brianne stared at him for a minute before she spun on her heel and strode along the corridor to the gate. When the guard turned at the sound of her footsteps, she said, "I'm finished here now." She should have brought someone with her. Someone who could have backed her up about Macklyn's lies. But he probably would've said nothing if she hadn't been alone. She stepped through the gate and waited for the guard to lock it again. She'd talk to her grandfather and see what he had to say.

Chapter Fifty

Talon

Talon sat on Ailis' balcony, Brianne against his side, their shoulders pressed together, his wings retracted. Ailis was inside, having been with Brianne when she went to see Briant. As he listened to her speak about her visit with Macklyn, he wanted to pound him into the red dust that seemed to be everywhere in Caelis. "What did your grandfather say when you told him?"

"He said not to worry about Macklyn since the poor kid, his words, was feeling terrible about being duped by Elden. That I couldn't expect him to have realised Elden was the enemy when no one else did."

"Are they keeping him locked up?"

Brianne nodded. "Grandad said he'd be in there for as long as they deemed it necessary."

"How long is that?"

She shrugged. "I have no idea."

He slid his arm around her waist. "It doesn't matter. If he tries anything when they let him out, we'll be ready." He grinned as he felt the tug of pressure at his back. "And I haven't seen anything from him to be worried about."

Brianne laughed, tilting her head to look up at him. "You think you can fly better than him now?"

Before Talon could answer, Marshall called up from the base of the four storey high tower, "Hey, bird-boy."

Talon looked over the edge to see Marshall grinning at him. He grinned back. "What, dirt walker?"

"You going to come down here or do I have to keep yelling at you?"

Talon turned to Brianne. "Coming down?"

"Sure."

Grin still in place, he tightened his grip around her waist, his other arm encircling her as he slid them over the edge of the balcony, his wings snapping out to glide them to the ground. He made a perfect landing, folding in his wings.

"What are you trying to do? Kill us?" Brianne stayed in his arms.

"This from the girl who throws herself off walls?"

"Shh." Brianne glanced upwards.

Talon laughed, guessing she didn't want her mother knowing about that incident. Leaving only one arm around Brianne, he turned to Marshall. "What's up, dirt walker?" His tone didn't contain the derision it did when he called Bellamy that.

"I'm heading home tomorrow, are you coming?"

"I don't know." Talon was torn. Brianne had talked about him watching out for her when she had the operation, but what about before then. And after? "Brianne?" He had no idea what question to ask, other than to make a question of her name.

"On horseback?" There was a tone to her voice that made it sound like it was as bad as a one way trip to the Infernal World.

"I can fly you there," Talon suggested.

"You don't have to decide this minute. I don't leave till daybreak. And if you aren't leaving, I can take a letter back to Garnet with me if you want," Marshall said.

"Thanks." He wanted to say more, but how did you tell someone you appreciated them being there for you even when you kept pushing them away. Even Marshall's parents were there for him, taking Garnet in while he chased after enemies. "I'll let you know tonight." He held Marshall's gaze until his friend nodded.

"I'll see you later then."

Talon watched as Marshall walked away.

"Do you want to go home with him?" Brianne asked.

Talon shrugged. "I don't really want to travel by horse, but there are still some Prilonians attacking travellers. It's going to take time to capture all of them. I could probably do aerial sweeps of the land and make sure they aren't attacked."

"That sounds good. Need an extra pair of eyes?"

"Absolutely." It was all he could do not to grin like an idiot.

"I'm only coming as long as I don't get stuck riding."

Talon nodded.

"And after we see your mate home we go to Iralen and see the doctors."

Joy burst through him, but he only nodded again.

"And I need a lift home, even though you can't fly." Brianne glanced upwards.

Talon grinned. "Can't fly, huh?" He pulled her close, his arms wrapping around her waist as he launched into the air, his gaze meeting hers. He hovered above the balcony.

"Don't let my grandad catch you flying me around like this. He'll lecture you for hours about how dangerous it is."

"Dangerous? Then I guess we should be grateful we're still alive."

Brianne laughed. "Absolutely."

Taking her repetition of his earlier answer as a yes, his lips met hers. He lowered them to the balcony, his wings folding in as one of his hands rose to the middle of her back. The sound of wings and a rush of air drew Talon slightly away from Brianne and he swore under his breath as he saw her grandfather join them on the balcony. He bit back another curse as Brianne pulled completely away from him.

"I'll get ready." Brianne disappeared inside with a smile and a hello for her grandfather.

"Fly with me." Briant didn't wait for an answer, but rose into the air.

With a glance at the doorway Brianne had disappeared through, Talon took to the air, speeding up to come alongside Briant. He waited for the man to speak, but he remained silent. They eventually reached Briant's house and Talon landed on the balcony next to Briant, a guard by the door.

"Inside." Briant gestured for Talon to go ahead.

Talon hesitated a moment, wondering what was

going on. There was only one way to find out. He preceded Briant to his study and stood across from the desk when Briant sat down. They had the room to themselves.

"I've talked to my granddaughter about joining one of four special teams we're creating that will be a mix of all our people. She said she needed to think about it and it wouldn't be until she's had that operation the rebel told her about."

Talon nodded, still wondering where the conversation was leading.

"I want you to talk to her. She doesn't need to risk herself on some operation that may not even work. She'll be out of action for ages. We need to be part of rebuilding our nations."

"No."

"What?"

"I won't ask that of her. And you shouldn't either." Didn't he know how important wings were for Brianne? Hadn't she done enough for everyone by risking her life as a spy?

"And why shouldn't I?"

"Because she deserves wings."

"I'm not saying she shouldn't get the operation in the long run. Just not now. There's still too much to settle. When things have been sorted out and when we know more about the operation, then she can have it."

Talon shook his head. "No. She deserves wings now. Not years in the future."

Briant stared at him for several minutes, silent. "I want you to lead one of the teams with her."

"Lead? As in co-captain?" He willed the man to say yes.

"No. Not captains, these teams will be separate from the armies. They will answer only to First Officers, Generals and Political Leaders. They'll be involved in policing the armies and ensuring each race abides by the laws and treaties agreed upon. These teams will be considered as one of the highest military ranks you can achieve. What do you say to my offer? With all you've done to help free our people you deserve it."

He wanted to say yes. Desperately wanted to say yes. "Is this offer only available if Brianne takes it up too?"

Briant nodded.

He couldn't. As much as he wanted that position, he wouldn't convince Brianne to give up her wings. "Thank you, but no." He started for the door.

"We'll want monthly reports," Briant said.

Talon stopped. He'd been certain he'd said no. As

much as he'd wanted to say yes, he was sure he hadn't. He turned to face Briant. "I turned your offer down. Brianne is having the operation."

"I know. You'll protect her while she's recovering and make sure the team functions without her until she can help you lead it."

His eyes narrowed. "What would you have done if I'd said yes?"

"Known that you wouldn't be the one to protect my granddaughter. I would have found someone else to protect her."

"And what if I still say no?"

Briant chuckled. "You won't. You might be annoyed with my test, but you're not an idiot. Besides, your friend Bellamy will be in one of the teams."

"Not mine." He didn't think he could put up with Bellamy permanently.

"No. He'll co-lead another team." Briant rose. "Tell Brianne. I expect the two of you to be at the middle garrison in two weeks. Being the first team, that will be your base. It will also be where all the teams gather for planning. Off you go." He waved towards the door.

Talon had so many questions to ask that he continued to stand in front of the desk.

"Go on." Briant gestured towards the door again. "All your questions will be answered at your first meeting."

Talon nodded, deciding to tell Marshall that he'd travel with him the next day before he told Brianne what her grandfather had offered them. It certainly wasn't the unit captaincy he'd strived for his entire life. No, it sounded a lot better than that.

Chapter Fifty-One

Brianne

Brianne reached for the next handhold only to find her hand flat against the top of the stone pillar. She pulled herself over the edge to sit facing the fortified city and castle. She was still able to climb to the top of her favourite pillar. Some things had changed in the past year, but that hadn't. Dusting off her hand, she reached up to tuck several loose strands of her hair back into the short stubby braid that barely reached her shoulders.

Her city was now no longer home only to Caelians. Several lowset dwellings had sprung up amongst the towers for the Terstens who had chosen to move there. Even some of the rebels, mostly Eriens, had moved in. There was also a handful of Prilonians living in the city, people who had disliked slavery and some who had occasionally helped slaves escape over the years. Bands of Prilonians still preyed on travellers, but they were becoming rare. Many of the Prilonians who had been rounded up had chosen to take a ship back to their homelands and the rest of the towns had been freed including the slaves. Much to Marshall's relief, his sister had been found unharmed at one of the cities furthest from the capital.

One other thing hadn't changed. Macklyn was still imprisoned even though he and his friends and family had repeatedly asked for him to be released. Their requests had been denied.

Brianne's gaze was drawn to the winged figure that came over the city wall, in the distance, headed in her direction. A smile curved her lips and she leaned back, resting her palms in the dirt to take her weight. She was glad Talon had decided to come home with her on her visit to her family. Co-leading the team hadn't left her much time to return home. She regularly saw her grandfather who had taken a more active role in the joining of their nations, but it had been months since she'd seen her mother and uncle.

Talon landed on top of the pillar, retracting his wings. "I've been looking for you for hours. Your mother said I might find you here."

Brianne rose to her feet, dusting off her hands on the seat of her trousers. "I wanted to see if I could still climb it."

"Why?"

She shrugged. "I don't know. I guess I don't want to forget how." She reached out for him, sliding her arms around his waist to draw him close. "Some things need to be practised regularly so you don't forget how to do them."

Talon grinned. "Like showing how grateful you are to be alive?"

Brianne laughed, brushing her lips across his. "Isn't facing death first a requirement for that?"

"No problem." Talon pulled away from her, taking her hand as he jumped off the pillar, dragging her with him.

The ground rushed towards Brianne and with a grin, she pulled away from Talon, her wings snapping out at the same moment as his. She beat her pure white wings, soaring towards the top of the wall that ran around the city, Talon at her side.

Free Ebook

Subscribe to Avril's newsletter to receive a free ebook. This ebook is exclusive to those on her mailing list. To find out more about this offer visit: http://www.avrilsabine.com/free-ebook/

*

We value your privacy and will not sell, rent, exchange or loan your email address to third parties. Your information is confidential and you are under no obligation to remain on the mailing list and can unsubscribe at any time.

Acknowledgements

Thank you to all my beta readers and editors, especially Mum, Caitlyn and Lloyd. Your help is invaluable.

To The Reader

If you enjoyed this book, why not consider leaving a review to help other readers discover it too? Reader engagement is one of the few ways that lets an author know readers want more books in a particular series or genre. So leave a review and tell friends, not only about this book but also about other ones you've enjoyed, so you can continue to enjoy books by your favourite authors for years to come.

Dreams are meant to be lived,

Avril.

About The Author

Avril is an Australian author who lives with her family on acreage in South East Queensland. She writes mostly young adult speculative fiction, but has been known to dabble in other genres. You can find more information about her at her website www.avrilsabine.com where you can subscribe to her newsletter to be kept informed about new releases, current projects, blog posts and exclusive news.

Titles By Avril Sabine

Stories about strong characters and characters who discover their strength.

SERIES

Assassins Of The Dead- Young Adult Fantasy/ Paranormal

Book 1: Dark Blade

Book 2: Dragon Touched

Book 3: Society Against Vampires

Book 4: King's Request

Dragon Blood- Young Adult Urban Fantasy (with elements of romance)

(5 book series)

Book 1: Pliethin

Book 2: Wyvern

Book 3: Surety

Book 4: Knight

Book 5: Mage

Dragon Mage- Young Adult Urban Fantasy (with elements of romance)

(Series two of Dragon Blood series)

Book 1: Promise

Dragon Blood Chronicles- Young Adult Urban Fantasy (with elements of romance)

(Companion series to Dragon Blood)

Book 1: Oath

Book 2: Betrayed

Guardians Of The Round Table- Young Adult Fantasy LitRPG

(Co-written with Storm and Rhys Petersen)

Book 1: Dexterity Fail

Book 2: Goblin Boots

Book 3: Singed Feathers

Book 4: Frog Mage

Book 5: Crystal Mine

Book 6: Cursed Harp

Rosie's Rangers- Young Adult Western Steampunk

(6 book series)

Book 1: Justice

Book 2: Vengeance

Book 3: Treachery

Book 4: Accused

Book 5: Wanted

Book 6: Corruption

Mark Of Kings- Children's Fantasy

(Upper middle grade/preteen)

(4 book series)

Book 1: The Arena

Book 2: The Island

Book 3: The Assassin

Book 4: The King

STAND ALONE SERIES

*Demon Hunters- Young Adult Urban Fantasy/
Horror (with elements of romance)*

Book 1: Blood Sacrifice

Book 2: Retribution

Book 3: Tainted

Book 4: Premonition

Book 5: Cursed

Book 6: Feud

Book 7: Extrication

Plea Of The Damned- Young Adult Urban Fantasy/Paranormal

(6 book series)

Book 1: Forgive Me Lucy

Book 2: Forgive Me Aiden

Book 3: Forgive Me Jena

Book 4: Forgive Me Kobe

Book 5: Forgive Me Marti

Book 6: Forgive Me Dawson

Realms Of The Fae- Young Adult Urban Fantasy (with elements of romance)

The Sword (short story in Like A Girl Anthology)

Heart Of Stone

Book 1: A Debt Owed

Book 2: Marked By The Hunt

Book 3: The Magic Collector

Book 4: An Unexpected Betrayal

Book 5: Imprisoned By Iron

Fairytales Retold (Short Stories)

Snow-White And Rose-Red

The Twelve Brothers

The Light Princess

Beauty And The Beast

Sleeping Beauty

Aschenputtel

The Golden Bird

The Frog Prince

The Death Of Koshchei The Deathless

Myths And Legends Retold (Short Stories)

Ion, Son Of Apollo

Sir Gawain And The Maid With The Narrow Sleeves

Princess Ilse, The Giant's Daughter

YOUNG ADULT NOVELS

Young Adult Fantasy (with elements of romance)

Elf Sight

Earth Bound

Young Adult Urban Fantasy

Stone Warrior (with elements of romance)

The Jungle Inside

Young Adult Contemporary (with elements of romance)

Through Your Eyes

The Ugly Stepsister

Perfect Little Princess

Young Adult Contemporary/Paranormal

Whispers In The Dark (with elements of romance and same sex relationships)

Over Too Soon (with elements of romance)

Young Adult Sci-Fi

Experiment X-One-Six (Urban Sci-Fi/Superheroes)

An Endless Dawn (Post Apocalyptic Sci-Fi)

CHILDREN'S BOOKS

Dragon Lord (Preteen/early teens) (Fantasy)

The Irish Wizard (Upper middle grade) (Urban Fantasy)

SHORT STORIES

Urban Fantasy

Eternally Late

Dealings With Joe

Glimpses (short story in That Moment When Anthology)

Contemporary

The Brat Next Door

Fantasy LitRPG

(Set in the same world as Guardians Of The Round Table Series)

Tales Of Inadon 1: The Disc (Co-written with Storm and Rhys Petersen) (short story in Game On! Anthology)

Post Apocalyptic Sci-Fi

Compulsive Directive

NONFICTION

A Year Of Weekly Writing Exercises (Creative Writing)

Cooking For Families With Allergies (Cooking) (Co-written with Storm Petersen)

Tell Me A Story, Grandma (Memoir)

For the most up to date details on available titles visit:

www.avrilsabine.com/books/bibliography

Disclaimer

This is a work of fiction. Names, characters, businesses, places, events and incidents are either the products of the author's imagination or used in a fictitious manner. Any resemblance to actual persons, living or dead, or actual events is purely coincidental.